THE TEXAS

All the news that's b...

Search for $50 Million D... ...y Continues

Federal agent Devin Kincaid arrived on the massive Fortune estate this week to spearhead the kidnapping case of the century. Baby snatchers have stumped local law enforcers, and pitiful progress has been made as to the whereabouts of "golden child" Bryan Fortune, who vanished from his bassinet into thin air two months ago.

Sources report that Vanessa Fortune, aunt to missing Bryan, is playing right-hand gal to the rugged Kincaid. But can this intense "older man" keep his mind on the case if his hands are investigating a certain feisty heiress? Maybe this big gun

is shooting for a promotion, as in Special Agent Son-In-Law....

Forget about Kincaid's roaming hands—looks as if family patriarch Ryan Fortune is *sitting* on his. Maybe to prevent himself from wringing the neck of his estranged wife, Sophia. Will this be the year that Ryan breaks the shackle on that fourteen-karat, diamond-studded ball and chain?

About the Author

LAURIE PAIGE

has received numerous awards in her fifteen-year
career as a romance writer, including a *Romantic
Times Magazine* Award for Best Silhouette Romance
and one for Best Silhouette Special Edition, plus the
Affaire de Coeur Readers' Choice Silver Pen Award
for Favorite Contemporary Author. She has been a
finalist twice for the Romance Writers of America's
RITA Award, presented for excellence in romantic
fiction. She and her husband toured the West looking
for their dream home. She found lots of romantic
locales for stories, before settling in Northern
California.

Look for these upcoming titles by Laurie Paige:
A FAMILY HOMECOMING
on sale December 1999
Silhouette Special Edition

MAKE WAY FOR BABIES
on sale April 2000
Silhouette Special Edition

The Baby
Pursuit
LAURIE PAIGE

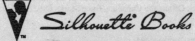

Published by Silhouette Books
America's Publisher of Contemporary Romance

Special thanks and acknowledgment are given to Laurie Paige for her contribution to The Fortunes of Texas series.

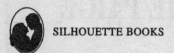

SILHOUETTE BOOKS

ISBN 0-373-65031-0

THE BABY PURSUIT

Visit us at www.romance.net

Printed in U.S.A.

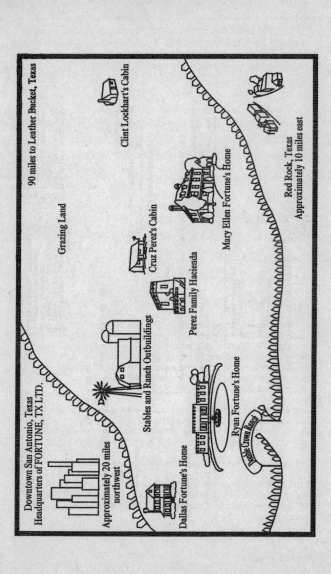

Downtown San Antonio, Texas
Headquarters of FORTUNE, TX LTD.

Approximately 20 miles northwest

Dallas Fortune's Home

Stables and Ranch Outbuildings

Grazing Land

Perez Family Hacienda

Cruz Perez's Cabin

Clint Lockhart's Cabin

90 miles to Leather Bucket, Texas

Mary Ellen Fortune's Home

Ryan Fortune's Home

Double Crown Ranch

Red Rock, Texas
Approximately 10 miles east

THE FORTUNES OF TEXAS

KINGSTON FORTUNE (d)

1st marriage
PATIENCE TALBOT (d)
└ Teddy §

2nd marriage
SELENA HOBBS (d)

CAMERON (d)
m MARY ELLEN LOCKHART

- HOLDEN ① — LOGAN ⑤ — EDEN ⑦
  m
  Lucinda
  Brightwater
  Sawyer*

RYAN

1st marriage
JANINE LOCKHART (d)

- MATTHEW — ZANE ⑫ — DALLAS ④ — VANESSA ②****VICTORIA ⑩
  m   m
  Claudia Beaumont   Sara Andersen (d)
  └ Bryan

2nd marriage
SOPHIA BARNES

- CLINT LOCKHART
  brother of
  JACE LOCKHART ⑥

MIRANDA
m Lloyd Carter (D)

- KANE — GABRIELLE ⑧

† ROSITA and RUBEN PEREZ

- Anita Carmen Frieda — CRUZ ③ — MAGGIE ④
                                    m
                                    Craig Randall (D)
                                    └ Travis

LILY REDGROVE
m
Chester Cassidy (d)

- COLE* ⑪ — HANNAH ⑨ — MARIA

James a.k.a. Taylor

- * Child of affair
- d Deceased
- D Divorced
- m Married
- *** Twins
- † Affair
- § Loyal ranch staff
- § Kidnapped by maternal grandfather

TITLES:

1. MILLION DOLLAR MARRIAGE
2. THE BABY PURSUIT
3. EXPECTING...IN TEXAS
4. A WILLING WIFE
5. CORPORATE DADDY
6. SNOWBOUND CINDERELLA
7. THE SHEIKH'S SECRET SON
8. THE HEIRESS AND THE SHERIFF
9. LONE STAR WEDDING
10. IN THE ARMS OF A HERO
11. WED TO A HERO?!
12. HIRED BRIDE

THE FORTUNES OF TEXAS™

 Meet the Fortunes of Texas

Vanessa Fortune: The beautiful virgin has rebuffed her share of money-hungry suitors. Can her true love come in the form of a handsome lawman just arrived in town...?

Devin Kincaid: The dedicated FBI agent thought nothing could ruffle him...until feisty Vanessa entangled herself in his kidnapping investigation. The tough loner claims the heiress is a royal pain—that he doesn't need anyone—but his tender actions tell a different story....

Maria Cassidy: The youngest daughter of Lily Cassidy is surely hiding something. What secrets lie behind her return to Texas and her sudden interest in baby Bryan's disappearance?

Cruz Perez: The handsome wrangler's motto is "Love 'em and leave 'em." But his bachelorhood is soon put to the test by an all-too-appealing new arrival on the Fortune ranch.

This book is dedicated to the romantic-at-heart: to Mary-Theresa, who told me she has an "old Irish soul" but I know her heart is forever young; to Jo in Illinois—yes, I have an idea for the children born in the Wild River series to have their own stories, but it will be 2001 before I get to them; to DL in Japan—yes, after almost fifty books, I still love to tell stories; to Rick, the bachelor—tomorrow the world!; to Heather, Holly, Jim, Kim and Nick— let's do the steepest streets in San Francisco again; to Natalie, visiting relatives in Italy—I cried for Sissy, too; to Leigh in London—hope the Russian translation went well; and to Clara in Kansas who sent the other verses for *Barbry Allen*.

One

Devin Kincaid swore and cut the wheel sharply to the left as the huge red horse broke from the trees to his right. For a second he thought the animal was a runaway, then he realized a slender figure was astride the beast.

His next impressions whipped through his mind at Mach speed—that the rider was female, that she was young and lithe of frame, that her hair, lashing across her shoulders with each lunge of the stallion, was the same shade of red as the mane that tangled with her locks as she bent low over her mount's neck...and that she was racing him!

He glanced at the speedometer. Fifty miles an hour.

The primitive urge to win at all costs surged through him. He pressed the pedal downward and felt the kick of the powerful engine concealed beneath the hood of the nondescript SUV push him against the seat.

The youngster glanced his way, then she urged the horse faster. Fifty-one. Fifty-two. Fifty-three.

The car pulled ahead, leaving horse and rider behind. A brief flare of triumph brightened the heat-laden August afternoon. It was short-lived.

Frowning, he wondered what the hell he thought he was doing, racing a kid on a horse at fifty miles per hour. If the horse had stumbled, if the girl had fallen…

Ryan Fortune would have his hide if anyone on the Double Crown Ranch was hurt because of him and a momentary foolishness left over from a childhood that had forced him to fight back or die trying.

He glanced into the rearview mirror but the horse and rider had vanished as quickly as they had appeared. Maybe he ought to tell Fortune that some ranch hand's kid was playing games with cars, probably on a prize stallion with a mile-long pedigree. On the other hand, a kid and her pranks weren't his main concern at present.

The baby kidnapping was.

With this somber thought, Devin parked under a tree a short distance from the ranch house, an adobe hacienda of both awesome dignity and inviting warmth. As he walked up the sidewalk along the green sweep of lawn shaded by the oaks native to the Texas hill country, he heard the pounding of hooves on gravel and turned to face the road.

The huge red beast bore down on him. He gauged the distance between him and the rapidly approaching animal. Energy poured into him as he prepared to dive out of harm's way. Six feet away, the rider pulled up.

The beast pivoted, then rose majestically on his hind legs, front hooves pawing the air. Backlit by the afternoon sun, horse and rider blended into one dazzling portrait of fiery splendor, so bright he had to shade his eyes, so alive and fierce and powerful, he felt an answering force within himself.

The rider studied him intently, and Devin felt a visceral thrill of recognition, as if he and the unknown young woman—she was definitely a woman, not a kid—had already met, as if this turbulent moment spoke of latent passions that had once flared between them...and would do so again.

She nodded once, as if acknowledging the mysterious connection. Then the great red horse seemed to gather himself on his powerful haunches before lunging forward into a ground-eating stride of unbelievable strength and speed.

Devin watched until horse and rider disappeared around the corner of the hacienda. At that moment, he realized his body was rock-hard and he was filled with an unquenchable hunger to follow wherever she led—

"You the FBI agent?"

He took a deep breath and fixed his attention on the man who stood at the edge of the lawn, looking him over with a critical eye. Ryan Fortune, patriarch of the Fortune clan, net worth one and a half cool billion, give or take a million or two, crossed the yard. He was dressed in typical cowboy work clothes— boots, jeans, long-sleeved shirt. A sweat-stained Stetson hat shaded his eyes.

Devin walked forward. "Yes, sir. Devin Kincaid." He shook hands with the rancher and sized him up.

The older man was muscular and tall, standing about an inch less than Devin's own six feet, two inches. Dark brown hair with gray sprinkled through it. Brown eyes. Laugh lines evident yet subdued by a deep frown that cut two creases across his tanned forehead. He looked as tough as whit leather, more the working cowboy than the rich man.

"It took you long enough," Fortune said in a low, harsh tone, the anger controlled but urgent.

Devin had dealt with families locked in despair. He understood the agony and the fear, the anger that tried to hide both but never quite succeeded.

"I checked in with Sheriff Grayhawk before driving out."

Devin knew more about the Fortune clan than the tight-lipped sheriff had revealed in his briefing that morning. Thanks only to lots of newspaper and magazine articles on the famous Fortune spread—the second largest ranch in the state—and to Sam Waterman, a long-time acquaintance who had a detective agency in San Antonio.

At the mention of the sheriff, Fortune nodded. The lines at the corners of his eyes deepened as he squinted against the sun and surveyed the area as if looking for the cavalry to ride up any moment, bringing his baby grandson back.

Seeing the man's expression soften slightly, Devin followed the dark gaze to the object of his attention. A young woman, dressed in jeans and a blue T-shirt, approached them. Devin recognized the rider of the red horse. The tightening in his gut said he knew her. Logic said they had never met.

Her eyes were as green as the grass he stood on. Her hair was tousled and as fiery as a Texas sunset. She was the promise of everything he'd ever wanted from life. Longing and lust raced through him in equal parts.

"My daughter, Vanessa," Fortune said. "This is the FBI agent we've been expecting."

"Devin Kincaid," Dev added. He held out his hand.

Her grip was firm, her fingers slender and warm in his. Though he couldn't see it, he was certain an arc traveled from the point where their palms connected all the way up his arm and down his chest to join forces with the primitive hunger she aroused.

Her eyes locked with his as an emotion flitted over her face too fast for him to read. She smiled briefly— as if in acknowledgment of the attraction, lust, whatever, between them?—her eyes never leaving his.

Devin dropped her hand as if it were the proverbial hot potato. He had studied pictures of the Fortune clan, but nothing had done justice to the vibrant life he sensed in this slender, shapely young woman. Her entire aura was one of subtle intelligence and willful spirit.

The youngest child—along with her identical twin Victoria—of a very rich man, Vanessa Fortune was twenty-five years old, a dabbler in psychology who had once helped the local police nab a serial killer. One lucky break, Dev mused, and she probably considered herself an expert on the criminal mind.

She was also twelve years younger than he was and as bright and shiny as a new penny. And as tempting to pick up and slip into his pocket. Ha. The Fortune heiress would be a pretty penny, indeed, for someone like him.

"It's a hundred and two degrees in the shade," the daughter informed them. "Let's go inside."

Dev followed her into the hacienda when her father gestured politely for him to precede him. He was aware of the other man's eyes on his back and had a feeling the father had correctly read his reaction to the daughter.

He wasn't here to get involved with a redheaded siren, he reminded himself sternly. Getting seriously entangled with any woman wasn't part of his future. Period.

The wrought-iron gate, wide-open in a friendly welcome, and tan adobe walls that had once protected the family from intruders gave way to a small courtyard that had been transformed into a garden of palo-verdes and native plants. Various-size stones had been used to effect a dry creek. A curving walk led to the steps to a massive wooden door with black iron hinges of conquistador design.

Inside was a typical great room and, beyond, an inner courtyard where the family would have entertained friends and often taken their evening meal in days of old. The courtyard, too, was an inviting expanse of trees and flowers, as well as a fountain and an overhead trellis covered with flowering vines. Under the trellis sat a cozy arrangement of chairs and an old-fashioned yard swing.

Crossing the great room, a dining room was visible to the left through a tall archway. Its glass-paned doors were closed. He surveyed the stucco walls and beamed ceilings. The house looked solid, stable... A good place to raise a family.

The wings on either side of the original hacienda had been constructed for the two sons of Kingston Fortune. However, Devin knew that Cameron, the oldest son, had built his own place near the main house after his marriage. His widow, Mary Ellen, still lived there. Ryan Fortune had stayed on in the main house. Dev wasn't sure where the ranch workers lived. But he would find out.

Just as he'd find out all the secrets of the Fortune clan and who would take the baby grandson and why. He had already concluded there was more than one person involved and that it was an inside job in spite of the many guests who had been present at the child's christening party. The grab had been too smooth, too easily carried out under the noses of the collective family members and their long-time friends and neighbors for an unknown trespasser to achieve.

"Iced tea?" the daughter asked.

At his nod, she used an intercom to relay the order—phrased as a request—to the kitchen and the many servants he knew worked there. The size of the ranch and its numerous employees might make his job a little tougher than usual, but not impossible. Criminals always made a mistake. There was always a weak link or an unplanned incident—

"Please, have a seat," Ryan Fortune invited.

Devin chose a leather chair at right angles to the matching sofa. From this angle, he could observe the entrance and the inner courtyard. He noticed a maid leave one room and enter another. She pushed a trolley much like those used in hotels. Another maid entered the great room, a tray in her hand. She served him first, then Ryan Fortune, who indicated the daughter should be next. Devin stored that bit of information away under "protocol of the rich."

The tea looked refreshingly cold. A sprig of mint and an orange slice decorated the rim of the glass. He wasn't sure if he was supposed to remove the mint and orange slice and put them in the saucer that came with the tea or just drink from the other side of the glass.

He picked up the glass and waited to see what his host and hostess did. They ignored the refreshment, each watching him as if waiting for a brilliant deduction, Sherlock Holmes style, on the kidnapping. Feeling distinctly foolish, he sipped the flavored tea, then replaced the glass on the saucer which, he noticed, matched the leaf design of the three glasses.

"How many men do you have working with you?" Vanessa Fortune demanded, perching on the arm of the sofa closest to her father, who had taken the chair that faced Devin across the coffee table.

He snatched a number from thin air. "Twenty thousand."

Dev didn't know why he'd chosen a smart-ass answer, other than the fact that Vanessa Fortune got his dander up. Among other things.

"I didn't mean the entire force of the FBI," she said, not taking offense. "How many from the district office came with you and how many from the local office are assigned to the case?"

"I'm it," he announced, checking both father and daughter to see how they took this news.

"One man?" she questioned.

Her lips tightened. The bottom lip was fuller than the upper, he noted, and she didn't wear a smidgen of lipstick. He wondered how that mouth would feel under his and was immediately irritated at the thought.

"The field office will supply any additional help I need," he continued. "For now, I want to explore on my own."

"Explore where?" This from the patriarch.

"Here. The house and ranch."

"That's about five hundred thousand acres," Ryan Fortune stated dryly, the impatience controlled but visible.

"I'm aware of that." Dev's tone was equally dry.

"What exactly are you looking for?" the daughter broke in. "Don't you think all the clues will have been eradicated by now? It's been two months since the kidnapping."

"I'm aware of that, Ms. Fortune."

"You had better call me Vanessa, otherwise you'll have several people answer when the rest of the family is present," she informed him crisply.

Devin caught the subtle nuance of arrogance in the correction, the demand that he do something *now*. He saw the father's gaze shift to her, to him, then back to the daughter. The man saw more than Dev wanted him to.

An uncomfortable flash of heat hit him someplace deep inside. He maintained an impassive expression with an effort of will. But the hunger didn't let up, nor the longing.

"My daughter will be available to answer any questions," Mr. Fortune informed him. "I've asked her to take you any place on the ranch you want to go. You will have complete freedom to investigate as you wish."

Another complication in an already complex situation. He ignored the woman and spoke to the father. "I understand Ms. Fortune is in school—"

"I'm taking a sabbatical from my studies," she

informed him. "A Ph.D. is nothing compared to finding my nephew."

He thought of days spent in her company. Fate had never been kind, not to him. "I don't have time for an amateur."

The verdant eyes flashed. "I won't get in your way."

He didn't argue, knowing the decision had been made before he'd appeared on the scene.

"You may go anywhere, question anyone, search any building," Mr. Fortune assured him. "If anyone gives you any trouble, refer them to me."

"Thank you, sir." Dev breathed a little easier about his job. With Fortune's approval, there was no doubt in his mind that he would get the cooperation he needed.

"Vanessa, take Mr. Kincaid to his room. He might as well get settled in—"

"I have a place in town, but thanks anyway," Dev quickly put in.

"Staying here will be more efficient," she told him in the same tone the father had used—as if no one would dare question the decision.

Before he could refuse, Mr. Fortune asked, "Are you by any chance related to the Montana Kincaids?"

"Not that I know of."

As if he were kin to anyone with money. He was willing to bet the Montana Kincaids were another rich ranching family. Maybe he should tell Mr. Fortune and his snooty daughter about growing up in the Houston slums with a drunk for a father and a beaten-down mother—

"I was in Vietnam with Wayne Kincaid. A good man."

"Yes, sir." Dev wondered if the older man's mind was wandering. People said and did strange things when they were under unrelenting stress for long periods.

"A lot of men didn't come back."

Vanessa laid a hand on her father's shoulder in a surprisingly gentle gesture that expressed, more than words ever could, her love for her family. For the instant between two heartbeats, Devin let himself wonder how it would feel to be included in that circle of love and loyalty, the inner warmth that spoke of family and forever...

"I'll take Mr. Kincaid to his room," she said, "then show him around. Drinks around six?"

Ryan Fortune patted his daughter's hand. "Yes. I have to return a call to my attorney. I'm sure you're aware..." He hesitated, then shrugged, his expression grim as he glanced at Dev. "It's common knowledge that I'm involved in a nasty divorce case. I suppose you're aware of that."

"I have the general details," Dev admitted. At the other man's assessing glance, he added, "Sam Waterman is a friend. He was in Intelligence when I was in the Marines." Waterman was now a private investigator and had been hired by Ryan Fortune to protect his family after the kidnapping.

Devin exchanged a glance with Fortune that spoke of common experiences, of friendships forged and proven in the heat of battle, whether that was in the jungles of Nam, the deserts of Kuwait, or endangered embassies in various parts of the world where he had served.

As an embassy guard who had figured out an assassination scheme on an ambassador before it happened, Devin had reported his findings to CIA Agent Waterman. The higher-ups had transferred him to Intelligence, which was how he'd ended up in the FBI when his tour of duty was finished.

"If you're ready…" the daughter said, making it obvious she was by rising.

Dev also stood. He thanked the tall rancher for his cooperation, then followed the daughter across the room to the covered and enclosed flagstone sidewalk that extended around the inner quadrangle and served as the hallway to the rest of the house.

"Except for the windows, this was part of the original structure. So was the great room, the rooms off it on either side and the wall enclosing the compound," she explained, seeing his interest. She pointed toward the back wall. "The stables are garages now. Grandfather—that was Kingston Fortune—remodeled the main house, enlarging the dining hall and installing a modern kitchen. Later, he added the wings on each side for his sons' families. This is my father's side. He and Sophia… He has a suite." She indicated a door as they passed.

Devin stopped. "I'd like to see it."

"Now?"

"Yes."

"I'll ask my father."

"He's already given his consent." He tried the door, then walked in.

The suite opened into a sitting room—a combination man's study and woman's parlor. An ornate recliner, gold-trimmed with red silk upholstery, seemed out of place among the obviously antique heavy Spanish desk and leather chairs. A white-and-gold table on spindly legs held a telephone and a pedestalled gilt mirror. The table and red silk recliner were placed so the occupant could view the inner courtyard with ease. The antique desk and two comfortable chairs, backed by floor-to-ceiling bookcases, filled the corner and wall nearest the entrance door. An open door revealed a bedroom.

Devin quickly inspected the area, including the adjoining bath with its whirlpool tub and fancy fixtures. He checked all doors, finding mostly closets—closets bigger than his bedroom at the house where he'd grown up in Houston.

"Okay, we can go."

"Just what are you looking for?" she demanded, the impatience—Dev thought it must be a family trait—visible in a frown that nicked a line between her eyes. She stared at him without blinking.

For a second he forgot the question and became lost in those verdant depths. He wondered what her passion would be like, if she would be as impatient to get to a climax as she was to get on with the investigation.

He reined in the hunger. A woman, especially this one, had no place in his life. Control was his strength; logic his métier. That's why he succeeded in cases that other law enforcement officials had given up on. Why he had been sent on this job—to solve a kidnapping, not to fall for the daughter of the house.

"What?" he said, vaguely recalling a question being asked, not sure if it had come from him or her.

She looked away. This time he sensed confusion behind the other emotions she tried to hide.

"Nothing." She led the way into the hall.

There were four other doors in the east wing. She paused at the first one and looked at him with a question in her eyes. He explored the room, checking it as he had the main suite. One door revealed a nursery.

The small room contained a combination dresser diapering station, a crib, bassinet and a rocker. There was a daybed—for a nanny, he assumed—and chest of drawers along one wall.

"Is this where the child was sleeping?" Dev asked.

She nodded. "Bryan. His name is Bryan. Claudia had put him to bed in here after the christening—" Her voice wobbled on the last word and she stopped speaking abruptly.

Devin sensed her distress and felt a tightening inside, as if what she felt, he did, too. This was a case, he reminded himself. He couldn't afford to get emotional.

"Okay, let's move on," he said, ushering her out. He glanced into the other bedrooms, noting that each had a door that opened to the inner courtyard, an ensuite bath, and the usual compliment of closet space the rich seemed to require.

The next-to-last door was her room. He smiled at the jumble of books, clothes, jewelry and other female "junk" spilling over the dresser, tables and chairs. The room was just what he would expect from a spoiled kid. This knowledge put her back on an even keel where he was concerned, and he relaxed somewhat, his libido easing up.

There were four doors in her room—one to the courtyard, one to a bathroom, another to a walk-in closet. The fourth door led to the room next door.

"Whose room is this?" he asked, annoyed by the connecting door and the possibility of having a lover close by, then was annoyed with himself for thinking of it.

"Yours," she said, her manner indicating it should have been self-evident.

He couldn't hide his surprise.

Amusement flashed through her eyes. "I thought this would be convenient since we'll be working together on the case."

For a moment he was tempted to kiss the arrogance out of her, maybe throw a little scare into the over-confident debutante for taunting a male she didn't know. He erased the idea with difficulty.

"I'm here to do a job. You get in my way, and you're in trouble," he warned, trying to find the right ground for them, a neutral place without emotion or attraction.

"I'm going to help. I've read every book that has been written on kidnappings like this one." She gestured toward the books littering her desk. There were others on the criminal mind, he noticed.

Stubborn, interfering female. He could see she meant business. Okay, he could handle that. He was a great believer in using whatever came to hand to solve a case. He would give her something to do to keep her out of his hair.

Passing close to her on his way to check the rest

of her quarters, he caught a whiff of her scent. He was reminded of the outdoors, of sunlight and the sweet, spicy scent of wildflowers, of wind and the fresh smell of the earth after a summer shower, of nature and the powerful thrust of the stallion she had ridden....

Unbidden, unexpected, the hunger swept over him, as strong as the tornadoes that bore down from the northwest, destroying everything in their path. He fought the battle and won.

This he understood. It was passion, no more, no less. But the undercurrents between them whispered of something else. In the nursery, he'd seen the vulnerable side of her, the love for her nephew, the worry and despair that had shone briefly in the depths of her eyes. His partner's wife had looked like that after they had buried Stan.

From those two, Dev had learned what a real marriage was supposed to be, the give and take, the sharing of the good and bad, the raising of their kids...

The pain hit him as it always did—rising from his soul, tormenting him. Love, he had discovered early in his life, was a hurtful thing. It lifted the heart on wings of hope, then dashed it to the ground, shattered and struggling.

"Why haven't they contacted us again?" Vanessa asked suddenly, interrupting his inner tirade of guilt and blame. She clenched her hands at her sides. "I should have looked in on him. I started to, but I let myself be distracted. Maria had returned and I stopped and talked to her. After that, I forgot to check on Bryan. I should have. I meant to..."

When she looked at him, the pain was in her eyes.

He knew that feeling and the guilt that went with it. He looked away, refusing to give in.

"If only I had gone to the nursery—"

"And done what?" he asked harshly. "Surprised the kidnappers and gotten yourself killed?"

Vanessa shook her head, angry with herself for failing her nephew. "I don't know."

She swallowed hard against the knot of emotion that filled her throat, the agony in her spirit. "He was so tiny. Claudia was good about sharing him. She let me hold him and rock him. He liked patty-cake. And funny songs. He was our future, the next generation of Fortunes…" Her throat closed and she had to stop for a second. "It's so difficult, not knowing if he's alive and well. Or if…if…"

"In ransom cases, it's in their interests to keep him alive," he said tersely.

"Help me find him," she begged, the despair rising. She instinctively knew this man would do his best to find the baby. There was something about him that she trusted.

No, it was more than trust. The moment she had looked into his eyes, had viewed the steadiness in him when he had faced her as the horse reared and pawed the air, she had known there was something between them, something deep and personal and eternal. She said his name. "Devin."

His hand clenched at his side. "Dev," he said, his voice dropping to a low roughness that both soothed and thrilled her. "My friends call me Dev."

She heard the reluctance in his tone. He had been trying to distance himself from her and the feelings between them. She knew that. He didn't want to be friends with her. He didn't intend to get that close. She understood all that in an instant, and it didn't matter...because she knew it wouldn't work. Whatever this was, it was too strong for denial.

"Hold me," she said softly. It wasn't a request or even an order. It was stark need.

He rammed his hands into his pockets. His glare should have withered any expectations she might have, but it didn't.

"Hold me," she repeated.

"You're playing dangerously, just as you did when you pitted that red stallion against a car. If you had fallen—"

She shook her head, cutting off the reprimand, and felt her hair shift around her shoulders as if it, too, sensed the restless need of her spirit. "I'd been watching for you. I saw you turn off the highway. I wanted to be here when you arrived. I wanted to be the first person you met."

"Why?" He narrowed his eyes menacingly. "Why are you so anxious to keep tabs on me?"

The question was meant to startle and disarm. It did neither. "I want to help with the investigation. The baby, Bryan—" She stopped and took a ragged breath. "He's so little, only three—no, four—months old now. An innocent baby. He'll be frightened. How could anyone take him?"

Tears filled her eyes. She stepped forward, reaching for him, needing the strength she sensed he could offer. She sighed wearily as she felt his warmth enclose her like a sweet, welcome embrace although he refused to touch her.

"Money," he replied, his tone hard. "That's the usual reason people commit crimes."

She laid her hands on his chest. She felt small and fragile next to his great strength, although she had never considered herself either. His breath sighed gently on the top of her head as he stared down at her, his stance wary.

"I'm not your father," he said. "I'm not here for your comfort."

When she didn't step back, he put his hands on her shoulders as if he would push her away, then paused, as if he couldn't bring himself to be cruel.

"There's compassion in you," she murmured. Desperation and despair churned in her. "I'm afraid. I know the chances of getting my nephew back alive lessen with each passing day," she whispered, guilt forcing the words from her. "If I had gone to the nursery, they might have taken me in his place."

She was glad when he didn't murmur the usual platitudes that offered scant comfort.

"If he's alive, I'll find him," he said in a deeper, huskier tone. A promise.

She nodded, her eyes never leaving his. "I know. The moment I saw you, outside, when you arrived, I knew—"

She stopped, the explanation dying on her lips. He bent slightly, then pulled back, a stunned expression flashing into his eyes, replaced immediately by one of fierce, angry control. And something more—a darkness that spoke of regret and a bitter knowledge of life that excluded anyone else.

"Yes," she whispered, knowing whatever they felt

toward each other was right, her and this dark knight with eyes like the morning sky.

He sucked in a harsh breath.

She realized with something akin to shock that she wanted him to kiss her, to act on the impulse he had subdued. Instinctively she arched against him and felt the shudder that tore through his big, strong body.

She barely heard his low curse as he backed against the door frame, taking part of her weight as she was thrown off balance. Her own breath became ragged and filled with an urgent need she'd never before known.

A roaring filled her ears. A Texas tornado, she realized vaguely. It was coming toward them…

"What the hell is going on?" a male voice said savagely.

Two

"Matthew," Vanessa murmured, reluctantly turning from the warmth. Coldness rushed in when Dev released his grip on her shoulders. However, her heart was touched at the haggard appearance of her oldest brother and she suppressed her own needs and fears. "Have you heard anything?"

Matthew brushed her question aside with the usual Fortune impatience. "I need to talk to the FBI agent. Where is he?"

Vanessa gestured toward Dev with her free hand. "This is Devin Kincaid."

"You know him?" Matthew demanded.

She saw the puzzled suspicion in her brother's eyes as he stared at them. She stepped away from the solid comfort of Dev's warmth.

"Yes," she said simply, and realized there was no need for further explanation. In her heart, she knew this man well. She'd acknowledged that from the first contact. A moment ago, touching him, it had been like coming home.

"We met earlier," Dev said, covering for her. "You must be the baby's father."

"Yes. Have you found anything?"

"Not yet."

The brother cursed and stalked restlessly to the window that opened on the courtyard.

"It must have been an inside job," Vanessa told them.

When the men looked at her, she realized there was a similarity between them. They both had blue eyes and brown hair, Matthew's hair being somewhat darker. His features were more refined, aristocratic while Dev's were rugged.

She thought Dev's nose had been broken at one time. He sported a thin scar along his chin. His eyes were watchful, his stance wary, alert to danger. There was goodness in him. Caring. A sense of responsibility toward others. Again she was reminded of Matthew and his manner at times.

Matthew had chosen medicine after watching their mother die of cancer. The FBI agent had chosen police work, another field that demanded patience and a protective, nurturing personality for those with idealistic traits. She wondered what forces had influenced his life and knew she wouldn't rest until she found out.

"Why do you think that?" Dev asked.

She sensed his reluctance to accept anything at face value. "There were too many people around, too many friends and neighbors who know the entire family, for a stranger to walk in, then out, with a child."

"On the other hand, every bedroom has a door leading into the courtyard," he pointed out.

"And from the courtyard, it's easy to get outside," Matthew added. "There's an exit through the original wall at the end of each wing, plus the old stable doors."

"If someone left the nursery with the baby, they could easily slip into any of the bedrooms if need be—" she conceded, pointing toward her door and the adjoining room assigned to Dev. "From there, it would take only a second to slip down the steps into the courtyard, around the corner and out through the gate."

"If everyone's attention was toward the great room balcony where Dad was proposing a toast, it would have been an easy feat," Matthew finished. "Especially since the trellis partially blocks the view."

Vanessa could read nothing in Dev's face as he listened to their theory of the kidnapping. The familiar frustration welled up in her. She wanted to do something...*now.*

"I'd like to tour the entire compound today. I want to know who lives where—ranch hands, family, everyone."

"Yes," she said, reining in the impatience in the face of Dev's calm questioning. His quiet, impassive manner was a facade that covered a man of deep feeling. She had sensed that in him when he'd responded to her despair.

Or was she overreacting to the situation? Her emotions had been on a seesaw since the disappearance.

The unfamiliar sense of helplessness, of being jerked around at the whim of someone who wanted to harm her family, swept over her. She turned instinctively to Dev, wanting the succor of his warmth around her once more. She paused when Matthew sighed, then clenched his hand into a fist.

"Someone called," he said. "I was in the doctor's lounge at the hospital. She said the baby was fine and that she was taking good care of him. Then she hung up.''

"Oh, my God," Vanessa whispered. "We didn't think of putting a tap on that line."

"Did you recognize the voice?" Dev demanded. "If you have any idea at all, speak up. Nothing and no one is too vague to be discounted."

Matthew shook his head. "The voice was a whisper. I could barely hear her—"

"How do you know it was a woman?" Dev asked.

Vanessa found herself staring at Matthew with the same intent look that Dev turned on him. She saw surprise, then doubt, rush through her brother's eyes.

"I don't know," he said slowly. "I just thought…it seemed to me…" He shook his head. "It could have been a man."

"No," Dev said. "A person's instincts are usually right. Something tipped you off, something too subtle to be recalled consciously."

Matthew continued to look troubled. "Instincts have been wrong before."

"So has reasoning," Dev said dryly.

Vanessa gazed from one man to the other. "We know one female who wants to hurt us." She didn't say the name aloud.

"That bitch," Matthew said, echoing her feelings.

"If you're thinking of your stepmother Sophia," Dev said, "why would she want to reassure you about the child?"

"So we would pay the ransom," Vanessa told him. "If Bryan is…" She couldn't say it.

"Dead," Matthew said hoarsely. "If he's dead."

"But he's not," Vanessa said quickly, unable to

stand his agony. "That's why they're keeping us waiting. They think we'll pay more if they string us along so we'll be more anxious."

"Would you?"

Vanessa frowned as Dev prodded and questioned, casting doubts on their reasoning. She and Matthew had discussed the case a thousand times. "My father will pay whatever it takes."

"Other than the original note for fifty million dollars and the one call, you've heard nothing?"

"That's right," Matthew answered.

"Where were you when the alleged kidnapping took place?" he asked Matthew.

Vanessa couldn't believe the implication behind the question. "Matthew didn't take his own child," she declared hotly.

Dev continued to watch Matthew with his impassive gaze.

"I was... After the christening, I stayed close to my wife. We were outside—"

"You were near the fountain," Vanessa added. "You and Holden were talking. Claudia and Lucinda were close by."

The blue gaze swung to her. "Where were you?"

"I was on my way into the house and saw Maria standing under the trellis. I stopped and welcomed her back. We talked for several minutes. She seemed embarrassed at seeing me. She wouldn't look at me. I think she was worried about facing her mother after leaving the way she did and staying gone so long."

Matthew frowned, his gaze on the middle distance. "I remember now. We christened Bryan with water from the fountain. Rosita said the spring that feeds the fountain is the life source of the Fortune clan—''

Vanessa stepped forward and laid a comforting hand on her brother's arm when he stopped abruptly.

"I think I could kill whoever did this with my bare hands," he said after a few seconds.

Vanessa had never seen her brother's eyes so filled with murderous intent. While her other brothers, Zane and Dallas, had often threatened bodily harm to her and her twin Victoria, who had tormented them about their dates, Matthew had always been the quieter brother, the kinder, gentler one, while they were growing up. He had comforted her and her sister when their mother had died, although he had been seventeen at the time, only five years older than the girls.

She was also aware that Devin Kincaid took in every word, every nuance of emotion that was taking place. For a second she resented his cool detachment. But he had a job to do, and she understood that. She wanted to help him.

"I have the guest list from the christening," she told him, adopting his business-like manner. "Do you want it?"

"Sheriff Grayhawk gave me a copy. He also gave me a list of everyone who works here at the house. I want to talk to those people first. Do you know who was on the premises?"

"Yes. With so many guests, everyone worked that day."

Dev nodded, then dismissed Matthew. "You'll leave numbers where you can be reached at all times?"

Matthew handed over his card after scribbling his cell phone and hospital numbers on the back. After he left the room, Vanessa went to her desk. She picked up the list she had been working on earlier.

"I want to know where everyone that you noticed was around the time of the kidnapping," Dev said.

"I've already done that." At his glance, she smiled grimly. "I do know something about criminal investigations."

"Huh," was his succinct comment.

He obviously didn't take her seriously. She stifled the urge to argue with him about it. He would, given time, she vowed. Devin Kincaid, tough FBI agent, would take her very seriously before they were through with each other.

"Let's go over your lists," he said, his tone patient, polite. Sergeant Joe Friday, on the job.

Cruz Perez was angry. Vanessa could identify with the feeling. She wasn't very happy, either.

"Who the hell does he think he is?" he demanded.

"The FBI," she snapped, in no mood to put up with his temper as well as her own irritation at being excluded from the questioning. Dev had set up office in her father's study and allowed no one in while he questioned witnesses. She had been relegated to the role of gofer as he finished with one person and wanted the next brought to him. She had no idea what questions he asked that took so long with each person. And no one would tell her.

"That's my mother in there," Cruz snarled. Cruz was the horse trainer at the ranch. His mother was the housekeeper.

As if she didn't know. Personally Vanessa had been shocked when Dev had handed her the list of people he wanted to question when he'd arrived back at the ranch first thing that morning. She'd also been miffed that he hadn't taken advantage of their offer of a room. Surely that would have speeded things along.

"If he thinks he can connect her or anyone in my family to the kidnapping, he can think again."

Cruz glared at her, his dark good looks dangerous and exciting as his anger erupted. However, since she had known him all her life—he was four years her senior—she wasn't at all worried or impressed.

"No one thinks that—"

The door opened. "Thank you, Mrs. Perez," Dev said in his even tone. His gaze went from the house-keeper, who had been on the ranch since before Vanessa was born, to slide over Vanessa and on to Cruz.

"I'll send lunch in," Rosita promised warmly.

"That would be kind of you." Dev spoke to Cruz. "Cruz Perez? Please come in. Thank you for coming."

The door closed in Vanessa's face. For the fourth time that morning.

Dev had first talked to her father at length and without her presence, then Ruben Perez, Rosita's husband and the ranch foreman, then Rosita, and now Cruz. She was nearing the screaming point—

"Come," Rosita said, her dark eyes filling with amusement. "He wants to have lunch with you."

Vanessa's chin dropped in surprise. "He does?"

"You know he does," Rosita said wisely.

She led the way to the kitchen where two women

busied themselves between the huge stove and wall of double ovens. The smell of baking bread filled the air as usual on Friday morning. By Monday, the fresh loaves would be gone and new ones would be baked to get them through the week.

The kitchen had been the twins' favorite place after the death of their mother. Rosita had taught them to cook everything from crown roast to homemade tortillas. She had also taught them that grief could be bearable when shared.

"Whole or half?" Rosita asked, referring to the loaf of bread she was slicing.

"Half," Vanessa said.

While Rosita prepared a whole sandwich for Dev and a half one for her, Vanessa arranged their dishes on a tray, including the salads and cups of tortilla soup for each of them. She wasn't sure if she should allow herself to be mollified at being included during lunch or if she should give him the silent treatment for not letting her take part in the questioning.

She sighed heavily.

Rosita poured tall glasses of iced tea. "Next time you have hot tea, I will read the leaves for you."

"Do you think you'll see anything?" As a child, Vanessa had always wanted to know the future.

The housekeeper had finally told her she was a very mysterious person and nothing could be seen in her future, except that it would be fun and filled with adventure.

But that had been Victoria's future. Her twin, a pediatric nurse, was the one off on an adventure, teaching health and helping children on some tiny island republic off the coast of South America. Vanessa liked things closer to home.

Carefully carrying the tray back to the study, Vanessa had a sudden yearning to see her twin and confide all the hopes and misgivings of her heart. Only Victoria would understand completely…

"Come in," Dev called when she tapped the door with the toe of her shoe.

"I can't open the door," she muttered, and heard the note of complaint in her tone. Right. How to win friends and influence your enemies: be a grouch.

The heavy portal opened. She entered the study. "Clear the desk," she ordered.

He stacked his papers neatly to one side. She balanced the tray on the corner of the desk and spread the feast on the open space. She pulled the chair to the side and took her place. Dev took his position behind the desk.

"You look quite at home there," she told him. "My father might get jealous. The lord of the manor used to sit there and dole out justice to my brothers and us."

"Us?" he said.

"Victoria and myself."

"You were always a pair?"

"Of course. We were twins. What one did, the other did, too." She grinned. "We thought we had it all worked out when we decided that one of us should study for the biology test and the other for English finals when we entered high school. Since we had been assigned to different classes, we thought we could simply swap and each take the same test twice."

"Did it work?"

"Yes." She grimaced. "But about halfway through our freshman year, the English teacher caught on when someone spilled milk on Victoria. My dress was dry when I went in to take the test right after lunch. My dad grounded us for the entire semester after that."

"Tough," he said. He even looked sympathetic as well as amused. He took a bite out of his sandwich.

Vanessa ate, too, aware of the quiet that surrounded them. Her father was in town, probably visiting Lily. Matthew and Claudia had moved out of their house in town and back to the ranch to escape the prying eyes of the paparazzi who had hounded them since the kidnapping. There was still speculation on prime time news about the situation. The couple had taken up residence in the wing formerly occupied by Uncle Cameron's family before he and Aunt Mary Ellen had built their own house.

"Why isn't Savannah Clark's name on the list?" Dev asked, breaking into her musings.

"I forgot about her," Vanessa admitted. "She wasn't on the guest list for the christening since I had invited her down to visit with me for the week."

"Did she date any of your brothers?"

"Heavens, no. She and I were roommates in college. She didn't know my family before then. I wouldn't wish my brothers on any unsuspecting female."

He didn't seem to see the humor in her statement. His thick black brows drew closer over the beautiful summery blue of his eyes.

"She's a teacher in Dallas?"

Vanessa paused before answering. "Yes. How did you know that?" She reached for the list.

He moved it out of her grasp.

"Tell me about that day. Start right after the christening and tell me everyone you spoke with and where you were at the time. Picture it in your mind."

"Perhaps you'd like me to use self-hypnosis and regression?" she suggested, annoyed at his excluding her from his confidence, especially when she had already told him all she could remember at least three times.

"Just what you recall will be fine." He pulled a legal pad toward him.

He was being very distant and crisp with her this morning. It was a denial of the attraction between them and the magic of those moments in her bedroom.

"How did you know about Savannah?" she asked.

"The sheriff filled me in."

It was foolish to feel personally rejected, but she did. She knew this was an investigation. He was doing his job. Still, he could have told her what he had in mind.

The terrible despair she'd felt upon realizing the baby was really gone fell upon her. Her eyes ached with unshed tears. She took a steadying breath.

"Savannah and I stood directly behind my father and Lily…Lily Redgrove Cassidy. I forgot to put her down, too. She's Dad's fiancée."

"When his divorce from his present wife—Sophia—is final," Dev reminded her, his tone without inflection. He tugged his tie loose, then tossed it to the chair that held his jacket.

"Sometimes I wish Sophia would choke on a chicken bone."

Her comment brought a flicker of emotion to his eyes. It wasn't fair for a man to have eyes like that, Vanessa thought, eyes so beautiful they made a woman melt whenever he looked her way—even when he was frowning rather ominously, as he was at her right now.

"Just kidding," she added.

"I wouldn't," he said without a smidgen of a smile. "Things sometimes have a way of coming true, and then you're sorry for your evil thoughts."

"Were you?" she asked with sudden insight.

"What?"

"Sorry when what you wished came true."

His face hardened into a mask. "No."

"What was it?"

"I wished my father would die."

"And he did?"

"Coming home drunk one night, he ran into a truck. I'd wished for it a hundred times."

"Did he hit you and your mother?"

His hesitation was noticeable. "Yes."

She understood the darkness in him now. "It wasn't your fault. Your mother was the adult. It was her job to protect you, not the other way around. She chose to stay instead of leaving your father."

"That's easier said than done."

"I didn't say it was easy, only that she made a choice each time she could have left and didn't."

The muscles tightened in his jaw, but he didn't say anything else.

"You won't always close me out," she vowed.

"Don't confuse me with one of your psychology projects," he advised. "My life isn't open for study."

"I don't have to study it. I know all about you. From the moment we met. Just as you know me."

She could feel the closing down and shutting out as he gazed at her without speaking. It hurt. She looked away, suddenly unsure of herself.

"I know you as the pampered darling of a very rich father," he said calmly. "You're spoiled, impatient and probably think you were put on earth to tell everyone how to live."

"That's right. My twin thinks it's her calling to save the world. I tell people how to save themselves. We're a good team, don't you think?" Her tone challenged him to disagree with her.

He shrugged.

She finished her lunch, her eyes ever drawn to him. He glanced at her occasionally, noting her steady perusal, but obviously didn't let it bother him. He looked over his papers while he ate.

"Let's go for a ride," she suggested, overcome with a need to do something. She stacked dishes on the tray.

He stopped her from taking his soup. "I'd like to finish, if you don't mind. Besides, I've got work to do."

"Being outdoors clears the cobwebs. It helps a person think. There's a trail along the creek that's perfect." She eyed his brawny physique. "Between Dad and Matthew, we should be able to outfit you. Since you're too stubborn to bring your things out here and stay in your room."

He leaned back in the chair. "This may come as a

shock to your delicate system, but not every person is born with a silver saddle in the stable, so to speak. I've never ridden a horse in my life.''

Heat slid up her neck. Her face grew hot. "That was terribly rude of me," she apologized. "I did assume... Wouldn't you like to learn?"

"I see no reason for it."

"So we can share all the things we like," she said, taking her most reasonable tone with him. "I want to show you all my favorite places, the hideaways where Victoria and I played—"

"Hideaways? Where?" he interrupted.

"Along the creek. There's a bluff where there's an overhang. We used to pretend we were Indians and try to track animals through the woods. Cruz was really good at it. He could follow deer and rabbits fairly easily. Once he led us to a bobcat. My brother Dallas and my cousin Logan were with us. You should have seen us scatter when the cat snarled."

"Interesting." Dev picked up the list of suspects, or whatever he called it, and made some notes. "Was he ever jealous of your brothers?"

"Cruz? Why should he be?"

"He's the son of a hired hand. Your brothers were the landed gentry. It would be a natural thing, especially since he seems drawn to the land."

"He wants a spread of his own, but it costs a lot to buy land and start an operation from scratch. He loves working with the horses, and he's the best cutting horse trainer we've ever had. His mother, Rosita, tells him all things will come in good time, but he's impatient."

"Now that's a trait your family should recognize," Dev murmured.

She wrinkled her nose at him, then continued with her analysis. "Lately, Cruz has been moody. I think Dallas offered him the money to buy a small place near here to start a champion rodeo line, but Cruz got all steamed about it. He seems to have a chip on his shoulder, but I don't know why."

Dev gave a scornful snort.

"Cruz isn't the sort to carry a grudge," she assured him. She saw the doubt in his eyes. "You don't suspect…surely you don't think Cruz…he wouldn't hurt us," she ended vehemently, indignant for her childhood companion and friend.

"He had opportunity. He may have motive. That only leaves one thing."

"What?"

"The drive."

"Sophia has all three."

"Your stepmother?"

"Don't call her that," Vanessa ordered sharply. "She was no mother to any of us. Aunt Mary Ellen and Rosita filled that gap after my mother died."

"All right. Give me a motive."

"She hates us."

"She stands to gain more from the divorce settlement than from a kidnapping. Why would she jeopardize a sure thing for fifty million in ransom that might also land her in jail?"

Vanessa considered the situation. "You're right. Sophia isn't stupid, only greedy. Father has vowed she won't get more than the Austin town house and the allowance he already gives her. Which is more than enough for ten families to live on.''

"But is it enough for her?"

"Well, I used to hear them quarrel about it when I lived at home full-time. She says she won't settle for less than half his holdings.''

"A cool billion and a half."

"Not really. Grandfather set up a trust for all the grandkids. Dad controls everything, though. I haven't paid much attention to the legalities of it, so I'm not sure how it's all divided."

"Hmm," he said.

She thought she heard condemnation in the word. "What does that mean?" she demanded defensively.

"It means money has never been a problem to you, so you've never had to think much about it.''

The truth in his statement hit home. "It means, I would never think of kidnapping to get it. But others would."

"Exactly."

"Cruz needs money to follow his dream. I suppose you think everyone who works for us is a suspect."

"If the boot fits…" he said.

"You'll find the one who wears it," she concluded. She smiled beatifically at him. "I know you will."

"Your faith is touching," he mocked.

She shook her head and gave him a slow, deliberate grin. "Not faith, my love. You have more than luck on your side. You have me."

"God help us," he murmured.

Three

"You're looking good," Vanessa said.

"Huh."

She hid a grin. Dev had arrived at the ranch dressed in jeans, obviously new cowboy boots—the correct kind, not the ones drugstore cowboys wore—and proper headgear, which for summer was a white straw hat. It had a blue band and no eagle feathers, thank goodness.

He was a natural athlete and had adapted his movements to those of his horse, Rusty, quicker than most city slickers. He looked great on the big roan gelding, which was her favorite mount because of his smooth gait. She was riding a gray gelding who was alert and good-natured.

After a weekend of easy riding and some practice at jumping in the ring, on Monday she declared him ready for the trail along the creek up to her secret cave. As usual, that morning he had talked privately with her father, then questioned several ranch hands before telling her he was ready for their ride. If he was saddle sore, he didn't complain, but rode with the stoic nature she had learned to expect from him.

She sighed. Those first moments of meeting, the attraction that had nearly ended in a compassionate kiss between them, might never have been. He kept his distance. She felt thwarted and discouraged on all fronts.

Turning her thoughts to the task at hand, she led the way through the stand of oaks and around the alders that lined the small, rushing creek. Instead of soothing her as a ride usually did, she became nostalgic.

"My twin and I hid out here overnight one time. Dad was going to belt us for riding a half-broke stallion that Dallas said we were too chicken to ride. But Cruz said it was safe, so we did it."

"You trusted him?"

She twisted around in the saddle to face him. "Yes. I told you he would never harm us."

"Your unfailing feminine intuition, I assume?"

"Yes." She stared him straight in the eye, willing him to acknowledge the feelings between them.

He gazed at her without blinking.

She turned toward the trail, annoyed with him. "You won't always deny it."

"Yes, I will. Because there's nothing there."

"How do you know what I'm talking about if there's nothing there?"

"Don't try your psychobabble on me."

She kicked the gelding into a canter. This part of the trail sloped gradually upward in a series of rolling dips and rises. The gray jumped each low place easily. She knew the roan would follow their lead. She didn't pull up until the path ended at the rocky ledge leading sharply upward.

Finally she stopped in a small hammock surrounded by wild pecan trees and shrub oak. She and Victoria had sprayed the poison oak out each year so that the area was safe for them to play. Dismounting, she dropped the reins to the ground, leaving the horse ground-hitched.

Dev did the same.

"We walk from here."

"Which way?"

"Up."

He took the lead now, his gaze intent on the ground. He bent and studied the nearly overgrown trail and every twig and blade of grass. When they arrived at the overhang of limestone that formed the secret hideaway, he heaved a disappointed breath.

"Nothing," he said. "No one's been up here since the last rain. That was four weeks ago."

"After the kidnapping."

"Yeah. I thought the kidnapper might have holed up close by, maybe left a clue. But no such luck."

He searched the cave, looking over the tin tea set she and Victoria had brought up years ago. There was a tripod for cooking over a fire, an iron kettle, a skillet and a trivet.

"Who used this?" he asked.

"Victoria and I, mostly. My brothers did, too, before they discovered girls and dating."

Dev walked out from under the overhang and stood looking down the three-story drop into the ravine, where the creek ran swift and cold over the limestone boulders.

"A long ways to go for water," he remarked.

"Not really. Come on, I'll show you."

She walked around the ledge that narrowed as it curved past the shallow cavern. Up the trail a few feet was a water seep. She removed a pan hanging on a nail pounded into a pine and placed it so it would catch the drip from the trickle of water. The drops made a friendly patter against the aluminum until the water was deep enough to cover the bottom of the pan.

"All the comforts of home," she pointed out. "Are you ready for lunch?"

He nodded, his eyes searching the area above the trail.

She returned to the horses and removed food from the saddlebag on her mount. She handed Dev the chilled container of lemonade when he joined her. Back in front of the cave, she divided the food she had prepared for their picnic when he had requested the ride up the ridge.

"How many times have you done this?" he asked.

She weighed the question. "Jealous?"

A flush lit his lean cheeks. "Hardly."

"You are," she said softly, wishing he would admit it.

He snorted. She laughed when one of the horses did the same as if mimicking him.

They ate the sandwiches made from roast beef, sliced homemade pickles and spicy mustard, then sipped the lemonade from tin cups taken from a rocky shelf in hers and Victoria's childhood pantry.

Dev was aware of the quiet that surrounded them. They were alone for all practical purposes, and it bothered the hell out of him. He should have insisted that Cruz Perez or one of the hands show him around the ranch. Being with the daughter was too disturbing for his comfort.

Her gaze stirred something inside him—a place

where hope lingered, foolishly believing the promises that life dangled in front of a person. But he knew about promises, knew that, like dreams, they were never fulfilled. He had no desire to be around to see the glow die when life slapped her down one time too many. Then she would know, too.

He concentrated on the details of the case. He had a good idea where everyone had been located and who they'd been with at the moment of the kidnapping. He knew which people correctly remembered events and those who had been mistaken...or had lied. There were loose ends, of course. Not everyone was accounted for by someone else.

Maria Cassidy, for one. However, Vanessa had seen her in the courtyard at the probable time of the kidnapping.

Lily Cassidy, Maria's mother and the fiancée of Ryan Fortune, said she had spoken to Rosita Perez about serving the champagne for the toast, but Rosita thought that was before the christening, not afterward.

Cruz Perez was also unaccounted for.

The horse trainer had said he'd gone to the stable to check on a mare having difficulty foaling. Clint Lockhart, brother-in-law to Ryan Fortune through the rancher's first wife, Janine, insisted he'd been outside at the time and hadn't seen Perez at the stable.

Lockhart had a cowboy who could vouch for him, but the man had finished his temporary job the day before the christening and had been at the bunkhouse only an hour or so to pack up his belongings the day of the kidnapping. Lockhart didn't know where the cowhand was now. Perez said he hadn't seen Lockhart when he'd crossed the road to the stable.

One of them was lying, Dev was sure. Or their timing was off. The local cops hadn't been able to locate the missing cowhand to verify Lockhart's story.

He was at a stalemate.

"Have you found any clues?"

Dev shook his head, then went back to staring out over the land. In the vast pastures that spread beyond the creek at the foot of the ledge to the horizon, he could see hundreds of cattle grazing peacefully.

Fifty thousand head. Five thousand horses. Anywhere from fifty to a hundred cowboys, according to the season. But most of them were scattered around the half-million acre ranch, too far away to have been involved in the family's affairs.

When she laid a hand on his thigh, he nearly jumped out of his skin as lightning sizzled through his veins. He pushed her hand away.

"I've written a profile of the kidnapping," she said.

She pulled a slip of paper from her breast pocket and handed it to him. It was warm from her body and burned his fingers with the magic fire that came only from her. He forced himself to read her notes.

Well-planned and executed, indicating insider information.

Two people, possibly three or four, involved.

Leader is crafty and willing to play games for bigger stakes. Controls accomplices who are probably younger and willing to take more risks.

Someone used to children is taking care of

*baby and may have called Matthew. This could
be their weak link.*

Her handwriting was neat with evenly looped letters, but the impatience was revealed in the flying
slashes that crossed the t's and the dots that were near
the i's but didn't line up with them. There was
strength and decisiveness evident in the bold strokes,
a certain confidence that could edge over into family
pride—or perhaps snobbishness, although he admitted
that wasn't really true of her—in the tall capital letters, a gentleness as well as an unexpected vulnera-
bility in the rounded strokes. He would have known
it was her handwriting without being told.

And that her background was privileged, that she
was used to getting her own way and that she wasn't
for him, no matter what wild imaginings occupied his
dreams. He sighed and finished off the lemonade in
the battered tin cup.

"Let's go," he said, and stood.

She took the cups and rinsed them out in the pan
of water from the seep, then replaced them on the
rocky shelf. Every move she made was poised and
graceful. If he didn't watch it, he would stare at her,
spellbound when he was supposed to be concentrating
on finding clues. Vanessa Fortune wasn't good for his
investigative abilities.

She turned and looked at him at that moment. Her
eyes were tear-bright. "If we don't find him, Baby
Bryan will never know the ranch or how to ride. He'll
never know his family… He may never grow to man-
hood or know his first kiss…" She shook her head
helplessly.

"We'll find him."

"How?"

He looked away from her despair. "We start with everyone who had an opportunity. Then we assign motives, no matter how bizarre, then we see who fits the picture."

"We look for a pattern."

He realized she'd had enough psychology to grasp his thinking. "Yes. No one does anything out of the blue, as most people seem to think. There are plenty of warnings. In this case, the puzzle pieces are there. It's up to us to find them and put them together."

"So we start with opportunity and motive."

Her eyes brightened with determination once more. Something in him that he hadn't known existed, that had been tight and concerned each time he saw her distress, suddenly breathed easier. He pulled back from the emotional brink. "I start. You stay out of my way."

This time he ignored the way her expressive eyes darkened with hurt. He had a kidnapping and enough Fortunes to contend with to last a lifetime. He didn't need *her*.

Vanessa joined her father and Lily in the courtyard at six o'clock. She poured a cool glass of champagne and took a seat across from Lily. "How are things going for you?"

"Fine," her stepmother-to-be replied with a kind smile. "You look tired. Your father said there's nothing new in the case. It must be doubly discouraging for you."

Her father sat beside Lily on the swing and dropped an arm around her shoulders. Their glance at each other was filled with love and mutual concern. Vanessa felt tears well near the surface. She blinked them back with an effort and took a sip.

"Is Maria living with you?" Vanessa asked. "I meant to ask her out to visit, but with the investigation..." She gestured vaguely to indicate a lack of time. Or interest, she admitted. She had no time for idle social visits. Or Lily's daughter. She had never been close to Maria.

Lily looked troubled. "No, she's rented a trailer and is looking for a job, she says. I really haven't seen much of her since her return. She doesn't seem to want company."

"We can't control our children's lives," Ryan murmured reassuringly to his fiancée.

She sighed and patted his hand that rested on her shoulder. "I know, but parents always worry, don't they?"

"Yes."

Vanessa saw her father's concern reflected in his eyes. She wondered if he was thinking of Matthew and Claudia. The tension between them was thicker than cream. She would have thought the tragedy would draw them closer, but she knew that most parents who lost a child ended up separated if not divorced.

Her thoughts drifting, she gazed at the sunset sky above the hacienda roof. She wanted several children. At least four.

At that moment Dev appeared at the great room door with Rosita, who indicated the family gathering under the vine-covered trellis. Her father stood.

"Come join us," he called. "What can I get you?"

"Iced tea would be fine." Dev crossed the flagstones and greeted Lily, then Vanessa, in his courteous manner.

He was dressed in the FBI uniform of dark suit, white shirt and conservative tie. She hadn't seen him in hours, not since their excursion by horseback at midday.

Her father handed him the glass of tea.

"Thank you, sir." He stood until the older man was seated, then took a chair to her left, a careful distance between them. He was so damn polite she wanted to scream.

"You have news to report?" her father asked.

"Not anything significant. The cowboy who was here but left the day of the kidnapping hasn't been found. No trace of him on the rodeo circuit, which he said he was going to follow, has shown up, not under the name he used here, at any rate. Mr. Perez said the man hasn't done seasonal work here before. He didn't know who had recommended the cowboy. I wondered if you knew."

She watched Dev as her father explained that the new guy had been sent by another hand who usually worked for them during spring count and the fall selloff, but who couldn't make it that year. As usual, Dev's face was impassive while her father recounted the facts.

Finished, her father settled back in the swing and dropped his arm around Lily's shoulders again. The two were always close, she noted, touching each other, looking to each other for agreement when a decision had to be made. It was very endearing. She found she was jealous.

She wanted Dev to acknowledge their attraction. More than that, she wanted him to accept it and to be glad. She wanted the excitement of kisses and intimate glances and sweet caresses. She gazed moodily at Dev. Her dark knight.

He looked at her, making her realize she was staring. She quickly took a sip of her drink and pretended she hadn't seen his quelling glance or detected his obvious disapproval of her.

"So what happens now?" her father asked.

"I wondered if you would be willing to hire someone recommended by Waterman, a security expert named Quinn McCoy, to follow the leads on this cowboy? I'd like to find him," Dev said.

"You think he had something to do with the kidnapping?"

"I don't know. I could follow up on it myself, but I'd rather stay close. In case we get another call or letter."

Vanessa listened as her father agreed to hire an investigator to pursue the missing cowboy. When Matthew and Claudia arrived, both looking tired, discouraged, and hardly speaking, she felt her spirits dip lower.

"I thought I would take up the offer of a room out here. I would like to be closer to the ranch for a while," Dev continued after greetings had been exchanged with the couple and they were seated. "I, uh, could stay in the bunkhouse."

"Isn't your room satisfactory?" Mr. Fortune asked.

"Well, yes, but—"

"Then it's settled. You'll stay here. Are you available to have dinner with us tonight? It's only the family."

Vanessa was surprised when Devin agreed. She wondered why he felt the need to stay on the ranch. The answer came to her after she went to her room later that night.

To keep a closer eye on the family.

She watched from her bedroom while he walked around the inner courtyard before driving off toward town to get his clothing. Her heart beat hard at the thought of his sleeping in the room next to hers.

"Don't," she said softly to the errant organ. Getting ready for bed, she recalled an old song, something about knowing a heartache when she saw one.

"I believe Vanessa and the FBI agent are interested in each other," Lily said when she and Ryan were alone in the swing under the trellis with the sweet-smelling vine growing over it.

"Are you serious?"

"Very, darling." She touched his cheek. "A woman in love is attuned to these things."

He caught her hand and planted a kiss in the palm. "I'm oblivious to everything but you. I've missed you this week."

"I had things to do. I was worried about Maria. I still am, but she doesn't want to talk about her future, at least not to me."

"Kids. They'll drive you crazy if you let them. Did you feel the tension between Matthew and Claudia?"

"This is so hard on them. They need each other more than ever, but there are problems between them that aren't resolved." She hesitated. "There are so many things that can tear people apart... Maria thinks you're stringing me along. That we won't marry."

"Then she's dead wrong. I promise you this—we'll marry as soon as I'm free to do so."

She sighed and laid her head on his shoulder, believing him implicitly. "I do love you."

"And I you. I'll never let you go again, so make up your mind to spend the rest of your life with me." He turned her face to his and gave her a hard kiss of assurance.

She closed her eyes and tried to think only of the moment. But reality always intruded. "Sometimes I'm afraid—"

"Don't," he ordered gently, fiercely. "I'll be free to marry you soon if I have to strangle Sophia myself."

She shuddered and shook her head. "Be careful of what you say. Words can come back to haunt a person." From the corner of her eye, she thought she saw a movement. "Who is it?" she asked.

No one answered.

"What is it, love?"

"I thought I saw someone, but I guess it was only shadows. The wind has come up and the tree branches are moving around."

"It's time to go in." He pulled her to her feet. "I need you in my arms tonight. I'm beginning to get discouraged about my grandson. I thought we would have him back by now. Rosita tells me there are strange things afoot, but she doesn't know who is involved."

"I didn't realize you were a superstitious person," she teased, bringing them back to a lighter note.

"I've known Rosita too long to discount any premonitions she might have. She's been right in the past."

"I know. She once told me a snake has a forked tongue so it could tell two different tales at the same time. I should have listened to her. I let…others drive us apart."

He led her into the house and to his suite. "It doesn't matter now that we've found each other again. We have the future. Forget the past."

The sadness of past mistakes rose in her, of loving this man and leaving him because of her own stupidity, of listening to the lies of his brother, Cameron, instead of her own heart. She sighed deeply, recalling the pain of being young and in love and terribly unsure of that love. "If only we could."

"We can. We will. I lost you once. I won't let it happen again. I mean that, darling."

She looked away, unable to face the confidence in his eyes, the love reflected there. So much had happened during the years they were apart, things she would have to tell him about…someday. But not tonight. Tonight was for them. Sometimes she felt she had only the moment, that the next one would be snatched from her.

Perhaps she should ask Rosita what she could see in *her* future.

Four

Vanessa heard the outer door close. She opened the one between her room and Dev's. "About time."

He gave her a severe frown. "Does that door lock?"

"There's a sliding bolt on your side."

"Good."

Her confidence that together they would solve the case, that they would grow closer, dimmed and flickered dangerously close to blinking out. His adamant refusal to let down the barriers, coupled with her continued worry over Baby Bryan, gathered into a hard ball of pain inside her.

Stepping back, she closed the door and pushed in the button to lock it on her side. She took a deep breath, then another. For a moment doubts assailed her. Being one of the Fortunes of Texas didn't guarantee life would be roses and sweet wine. Once she had thought her father commanded the world, then her mother had died. She had learned even the Fortunes couldn't control fate.

And neither could she.

She knew she expected too much from life. She always had. "Without dreams and aspirations, what are we?" she asked softly of the closed door between her and Dev.

Troubled, she went to bed.

"What do you think?" Vanessa asked. With the new day, her low spirits had revived. She had decided to take matters into her own hands.

Sheriff Wyatt Grayhawk read over her profile of the kidnapping. When he finished, he looked up, his hazel-green eyes bright with intellect and interest. "Very insightful."

"I need more information in order to expand the profile."

"Hmm," he said.

She wasn't offended by his reserved manner. Like Cruz, Wyatt was part of her childhood. Six years her senior, he had been a friend and playmate to her brothers. She had helped in his election campaign for sheriff by delivering flyers and calling everyone she knew.

"What does Kincaid say?" Wyatt asked when she managed to outwait him for once.

"Nothing," she admitted. "He's like you, the strong, silent type."

"He hasn't mentioned other evidence?"

She perked up. "Ah, there is more. Tell me."

He smiled slightly. She grinned back and curbed her impatient nature.

Wyatt went to a file cabinet and unlocked it. He removed a folder. "We do have a bit more information."

He opened the folder and lifted a note enclosed in a protective sheet. It was the ransom note. The letters and words cut from newsprint seemed to mock her efforts at solving the crime. Disappointment washed over her.

"I've seen that."

"But did you see the date on the back of one of the words?"

"Date? No." She took the sheet when he handed it over.

One cut-out word was flipped over. On the back was the date and a few letters from the start of a word.

"April sixth. L. B. W-e-e," she read. She bent closer and studied the letters. "Why, this is from the *Leather Bucket Weekly Gazette.*"

"Very good," Wyatt said. "The note was composed at the motel on the interstate near the Leather Bucket exit."

"How did you find that out?"

"We had a lucky break. One of my deputies is dating the daughter of the motel owner. She told him about her father complaining about the damage people did to the furniture. Someone had cut slashes in a table and left a mess of newspaper scraps on the floor. I had just assigned him to check some details of the case, so he put two and two together. The cuts match the size of the letters and words cut from the newspaper."

"I suppose there were no fingerprints."

He was silent for a moment. "The maids do a good job, but we did find one latent partial print that we can't identify."

"It could belong to anyone who has stayed there."

"True."

She hit the heel of her fist on the cluttered desk. "Why don't they contact us? What are they waiting for? We have the money. If they want it, they have to tell us how to deliver it.''

"They will, but in their own sweet time. They're pretty crafty for criminals.''

"How do you mean?''

"Think about it. If you wait until everyone has given up and the cops and FBI guys have gone back home, there's less likelihood that anyone could set a trap when the delivery is made, especially if you don't give the family much time.''

"Whoever is doing this is patient. That makes it harder to catch them. They don't make many mistakes.''

"Neither will Kincaid. Sam Waterman says the agent is the most tenacious man he's ever encountered.''

She slumped against the hard vinyl of the chair. "I want to help, but Dev won't let me.''

Wyatt nodded. "He'll probably have my head on a platter for telling you what we've found, but since it came from my office, I feel justified in sharing it with you. You're sharp. He'll realize it sooner or later.''

He didn't insult her by saying the information was top secret. She was grateful for that. At least Wyatt had confidence in her, unlike a certain FBI agent.

"Well, I suppose I'd better get back. Thanks for your help,'' she said, rising and adjusting her purse strap over her shoulder.

Wyatt walked her to the door and opened it. "I'll keep you informed.''

She reached up and touched his cheek in gratitude, her faith in herself restored by his trust. Heading out, she ran straight into the icy shards of a summer-blue gaze.

"Dev," she said, gladness at seeing him upping her heart rate.

He glanced from her to the sheriff, then back. "What are you doing here?"

"She wanted some information," Wyatt said easily. "I gave it to her."

"On the case?"

"Yes."

Vanessa watched the interplay between the men. When Wyatt didn't back down, Dev shrugged. "I hope you know what you're doing," he said to the sheriff, ignoring her.

She decided she would have to be the aggressive one if they were ever to get anywhere. "I'm hungry. How about going to lunch? I'm buying." The latter was said to provoke him.

It did.

He gave her a glare. "I have business. If I could have a moment of your time," he said to Wyatt.

Vanessa set her mouth into a smile and left the county building where the sheriff's department was housed on the first floor. Outside, the sun pelted her with unrelenting heat, shining from a cloudless sky, reflecting off the mica in the sidewalk and concrete structures.

She stood on the steps for a long minute, her mind curiously empty as she tried to decide what to do. She could call any of her many friends in San Antonio and go to lunch. She could go back to the ranch. Or she could wait.

Choosing a seat on a concrete wall that supported

a patch of grass and an oak that gave her a bit of shade, she waited for Dev to reappear.

Dev stopped on the top step when he spied Vanessa. His heart did one of its annoying flip-flops. He strode over and clasped her elbow. "Come on. We have things to discuss."

Her smile wasn't lost on him, but he didn't let it sway him, either. He was damn mad at her and the sheriff. He led the way toward his car.

"My car—"

"We'll pick it up later," he snarled at her.

"It's my birthday present from my father," she told him. "Dad would skin me alive if it got stolen after I hounded him about it for four years."

Dev glanced at the expensive red sports car that probably cost more than every car he'd ever owned combined.

"I'll tell your friend, the sheriff, to put one of his deputies to guarding it." He whipped out his cell phone, punched in the number and left a terse message on Grayhawk's voice mail. "There."

"Thanks. I think."

He ignored her sexy glance and the white sundress that swirled against firm tanned skin a good three inches above her knees and concentrated on threading their way through traffic to the parking lot where his SUV waited.

Once inside with the air-conditioning turned on high, he headed out toward the highway and the suburb where his own modest home was located. He turned in the drive and stopped under an ancient oak that shaded half the roof.

"Where are we?" she finally asked.

"My house."

"O-oh," she said, a little hitch of surprise in the middle of the word. She climbed out before he could come around and assist her. "I assumed you were in a motel. I thought you were from Houston."

"I am, originally. I've been here a couple of years."

Devin watched as her green eyes assessed everything in the yard—the rock garden and pond he had built beside the tiny creek that flowed during heavy rains, the pecan and peach trees he'd set out around the house, the blossoms making the yard a wonderland of color in the spring. He wondered what she thought of it, then chastised himself for caring.

He unlocked the kitchen door and let her inside. The coolness of the silent house was welcome after the hundred and ten degrees outside. He watched her look around while he removed his coat and tie and rolled up his sleeves.

"Do FBI agents always have to wear dark suits?" she asked.

"It's part of the code."

"I figured it was. Is this?"

Before he could prepare for it, before he could get his defenses up, she stepped into his space, raised up on her toes, wrapped him in her embrace and kissed him.

He turned his head so she only caught the corner of his mouth, but it was enough to send spirals of dizziness washing through him. The scent of her hit his nostrils at the same time. Powder and perfume and shampoo—a scented soap, he chided silently, probably French and hand-milled—and *her,* the pure essence of woman, sweet and willing and passionate.

His for the taking.

His heart nearly exploded, it beat so hard. Blood roared through his ears. Desire spread in a tidal wave, effortlessly bursting through the dam of his control.

"No," he murmured, his voice a ragged moan of sound in the cool stillness of the house, an acknowledgment of the hot need in them.

"Yes."

It was the last thing either of them said because he kissed her back then. Her lips were honey, as sweet as a peach fresh and fragrant from the tree. Her breasts pressed firmly against his chest. He could feel her thighs, the beckoning warmth between them.

The roar grew louder.

She turned her lips from his, murmuring his name. He trailed kisses along her neck. His hands moved restlessly over her back, down to her hips. She moved against him so intimately, he thought his knees were going to buckle as desire washed through him in deepening waves.

"Your telephone," she gasped. "It's your telephone."

He lifted his head. As the riot of blood calmed slightly, he heard the muted ring of a phone. Angry at the interruption, he jerked the cell phone out of his pocket and pushed the talk button. "Kincaid."

"McCoy here."

"Yes," Dev snapped, recognizing the name of the man who had been hired to trace the missing cowboy.

"I have some information for you."

Every hair on his neck stood up at the detective's

words. This might be the break they were looking for. "Right. Go ahead."

"Your wandering cowboy was supposed to join a friend at a local rodeo in Wyoming and go on the circuit with him. He didn't show up."

Dev muttered an expletive. "We knew that."

"However," McCoy continued, "he called and apparently plans on catching up in a month or so, said he had business that wasn't concluded yet. The rodeo guy thought his friend sounded nervous or upset about something."

Business as in taking care of a kidnapped baby? Dev wondered cynically. Was the delay in collecting the ransom making the kidnappers nervous? "Sounds like our man might still be in the area."

"That was my thought," McCoy agreed. "You want me to keep a tail on the friend at the rodeo?"

Dev considered. "He seems pretty forthcoming. Ask him to call if he hears from the cowboy again. Give him Sam's number. I want to stay out of the picture."

"Will do."

After hanging up, Dev mulled the information over, adding it to the pieces of the puzzle muddling around in his brain. Collect enough pieces and all would come clear.

He had a sense of events coming to a head. He could smell danger, like the ozone in the air before a storm. He tucked the cell phone into his pocket and turned back to the young woman who waited in his kitchen as if she were at home in a modest house in the suburbs.

Vanessa smiled radiantly at Dev when he looked

at her. "What was the information?" she asked, eager to put it down on paper. She had a pocket notebook on the table, open to her growing profile of the kidnappers.

"None of your business."

The words weren't spoken cruelly, and she didn't take offense. "Yes, it is. I'm helping, remember?"

"No," he stated flatly.

"My father—"

"Your father isn't in charge of this case. I am. I want you out of it."

"Why?"

"You're a distraction I don't need or want."

"Oh, yes, you do want me. That's part of the problem, as you see it." She heard the stubbornness in her voice.

"What do you see?"

He gave her a narrow-eyed scrutiny, but she refused to be daunted. "I see us working together. You have the know-how of your years in law enforcement. I have the knowledge of seven years of study of human behavior. Let me work with you on this."

Her words painted a picture of closeness that he had never known. It stirred the old dreams he'd had as a boy—the happy family, sharing meals, warmth, love, things that would never exist for him.

"Yeah, we were really working on the case a moment ago. If McCoy hadn't called, we'd be in my bed right now, acting like a couple of jackrabbits in heat."

"Would that be so terrible?"

He shrugged. "I like a roll in the sack the same as the next man."

"Don't make it sound like a...like a..."

"A casual romp?" he suggested, his tone coldly amused. He had to get the notion that they could make it as a couple out of her mind. If he had to hurt her to do it, then that was what he had to do. "That's all it would be."

She held up a hand to stop him, eyes vulnerable, her mouth soft, trembly, kissable. "No."

"Yes." He leaned both hands on the table and looked her straight in the eye. "A quick—"

"Don't."

"You want it prettied up? I can give you sweet words. Tell me what you like. Endearments? Promises? I can do them. It won't mean a thing, but I can deliver. Just tell me."

"You're being cruel," Vanessa reprimanded him gently, sure that this was only another tactic to keep his distance. With the warm memory of his kiss still on her lips, she knew that wasn't possible. "You know it isn't like that between us."

"No?"

He reached for her, pulling her up and sweeping her into his arms. She stared at him, confused, her usual confidence dimmed into uncertainty.

He returned her stare, his face set and angry. It wasn't the ruthlessness she feared in him. It was the grim determination to show her that they didn't belong together.

"You're trying to frighten me," she said as calmly as she could, "but I know you won't hurt me."

He entered a bedroom. It was as neat and uncluttered as the kitchen. As if no one really lived there. That seemed terribly sad. She wanted to weep for him and the life he'd lived that had destroyed his trust as well as his dreams.

When he tossed her on the wide bed, she lay against the dark blue comforter without moving. If he wanted to keep her there, she didn't stand a chance of getting away.

When his hands went to his shirt buttons, her mouth went dry. He undid the first one, his eyes never leaving hers. There was no visible softening in his attitude. Standing beside the bed, with her lying down, he seemed bigger, tougher, blatantly masculine.

And in control.

She relaxed and smiled up at him. "It isn't your nature to intimidate women and children."

The bed bounced when he threw himself down beside her. "I'm a man. Don't ever forget it," he warned just before his mouth crushed down on hers.

He kissed her lips, her neck, the tingly spot under her earlobe. He left a moist trail of liquid fire along her collarbone and down the modest vee of her sundress. Her breasts beaded in longing for his complete touch.

"I won't," she murmured, running her hands through the thick, dark strands of his hair, delight replacing fear as passion flooded her body and warmth crept into her heart. "Kiss me some more."

He rested on one elbow, his eyes probing every thought in her head. "You just don't get it. I'm twelve years older than you. Do you really think I'm interested in a spoiled rich kid who's used to getting her way?"

"Aren't you?" she challenged.

"Only in one way." He stood and pulled his cuffs down. "And I don't have time for that at present. I have a meeting at my office in thirty minutes. It's time to go."

She followed him into the kitchen when he stalked from the room. "Why did you bring me here?"

He held the door open. "To show you my life, how it is and how it's going to stay. I'd like you in my bed, but you don't fit in anywhere else. Think you can get that?"

She nodded as they stepped into the heat of the August afternoon. "Yes, I get it."

The tears pressed closer to the surface. In her heart, she wept for him and the boy who had been so terribly hurt that he'd left his hopes behind.

He drove her back to the parking lot. Like him, she remained silent on the trip. The future seemed as dark as the thunderheads gathering on the western horizon.

Dev stood in the center of the courtyard. In black jeans, shirt and sneakers, he was nearly invisible. Everyone in the Fortune house had gone to his or her room. That was good.

He had been in residence all week, long enough for the family and the ranch workers to get used to him and go about their daily activities without paying him undue attention. Exactly what he wanted. He knew their routines now and could reconstruct the day of the kidnapping with a fair idea of the accuracy of his calculations.

As silently as a shadow, he returned to the building after exploring the garages and listening outside the doors of the servants' quarters. In the hallway that had once been open to the outside, he slipped along the flagstones and paused outside Ryan's suite.

For a moment he listened to the man's conversation with his fiancée. After a while he moved on. The older couple's talk centered on the oldest Fortune son.

At that son's door, the situation was more dynamic. Matthew and his wife were having words.

"I should never have married you," Claudia said.

"So why did you?" her husband asked in a snarly tone.

A drawer opened, then closed loudly.

"If we were an ordinary couple…if I'd married an ordinary man, not a Fortune, this wouldn't have happened. My son wouldn't be gone—"

"Dammit, he's *my* son, too," Matthew said in a raised voice. "What the hell do you want me to do? Change my name? Deny who I am? Forget my family?"

"No, I only meant… This is hopeless."

After a minute, Dev heard Matthew speak wearily, "For God's sake, stop crying."

"The baby… My milk has dried up."

Another minute of silence passed. Dev started to move on, his emotions carefully sealed off from the couple's troubles. He heard footsteps, then…

"Claudia…I'm sorry, darling. It will be okay. We'll get the baby back. You'll see…"

Silence.

"Don't touch me," the woman said.

"Honey, please—"

"No! Don't! I can't bear it…"

Dev ducked behind a potted shrub before the angry steps reached the door. He watched as Matthew left his quarters, headed down the walkway opposite of where he was concealed, then around the corner and out the side door. Dev figured the doctor was going for a ride.

In the short time he'd been on this job, he'd learned that was what the father, daughter and oldest son did when they needed to get away—head for the stables and a long ride on one of the horses.

After what he considered a safe period, Dev followed the doctor out the side door. He walked the half mile to the stables and arrived in time to see Matthew ride off across the pasture toward the line of trees beside the creek.

Dev checked on the Friday night activity in the bunkhouse. Four cowboys were playing a card game, four were watching television, and the rest were occupied at various tasks—writing letters, braiding belts, oiling tack or surfing the Net on laptop computers. The modern age had invaded the West.

He stood in the shadows long after Matthew Fortune had ridden out his frustrations and returned, after the few cowboys who had been off the ranch quietly entered the bunkhouse, after the lights went out at the other Fortune house where the widow, Mary Ellen, lived, and after Cruz Perez arrived from some unknown trip, checked the mares and foals in the home pastures, then went to his own small cabin nestled in a clump of cottonwoods.

At midnight, all was quiet.

He waited.

It was after two before Clint Lockhart arrived. Dev checked the luminous hands on his watch and suppressed a yawn. Damn, but he was tired.

Lockhart was in his forties, but he managed to lead an active social life, it seemed. So did Perez. For that matter, so did the several Fortune sons, both Ryan's and the deceased Cameron's.

One of the problems with the whole Fortune operation was that it was so wide-open. People came and went freely. Neighbors dropped in. Salesmen called. Attorneys, mailmen, veterinarians, girls ga-ga over cowboys and the Fortune name, guys hankering after the Fortune daughter—there was a damn parade in and out of the place.

Sooner or later, though, someone would make a mistake.

He moved silently through the dark toward the main house. Instead of returning the way he'd left, he entered the small welcoming courtyard at the front of the house.

Standing in the shifting shadows cast by tiny spotlights hidden among the plants, he studied the windows along the front of the house. It would have been easy to hand a baby out the window from either the bedroom or the study to someone who waited below, then that person could make a quick getaway across the lawn, past the oak trees surrounding the ranch house and into a waiting vehicle.

As easily as that, the deed would be done.

He moved silently along the wall to the door that led to the back courtyard. He stopped abruptly, aware of another person when he stepped inside the short corridor.

"What are you doing?" a voice whispered in the dark.

"I was restless," he replied to Vanessa. "I went for a walk down to the stables."

"Liar," she said.

He would have grinned except he was in no mood to deal with her. "Yeah. Look, it's late. I'm going to bed."

She followed him into his room.

"Do you mind?" he asked politely, holding the door open and hoping she would take the hint.

"Yes, I do," she snapped. "I mind very much. You're spying on my family. Why?"

He saw no reason to pretty up the facts. "To see who might have a reason to kidnap the Fortune heir."

Five

Vanessa was shocked. "In the family?"

"On the ranch." He folded his arms across his chest. "I agree with your appraisal. To take the child in broad daylight with so many people about, required someone who could cover for himself if he was seen with the baby."

"It could have been a woman."

"It could have," he agreed.

She eyed his dark clothing. "So, who have you been watching tonight?"

He didn't answer.

"Everyone," she said. "Including my father and brother. Then you went outside. I lost sight when you went into the shadows under the oak tree near the stable."

"That's pretty much where I stayed. I could see who came and went from the main house as well as the bunkhouse and other buildings."

When he sat in a chair and untied his shoes, then kicked them off, she took that as a signal that the conversation was at an end.

"Do you mind going to your room?" he asked politely. "I need some rest."

"I thought FBI agents never slept."

He watched her for a long minute, long enough to make her squirm, then said, "You're in a snit—"

"I'm furious. You think you know everything, but you don't know my family or our friends."

"Sometimes an outsider can see more clearly."

She sighed and changed her tactics. "I wish I could break through that wall of calm that surrounds you. I hate it when you sound so removed from it all when I'm ready to explode with frustration and worry."

"Emotion serves only to cloud judgment."

Tears pressed behind her eyes. "I know," she said. "In my mind, I know that, but in my heart...I need...more, but that's foolish. There can never be anything between us, isn't that right?"

"Yes."

"Thus the wise one has spoken." She couldn't hide the bitterness that welled inside her, adding to the pressure of the tears. "But I feel so sad."

He stood abruptly and took her by the arm. "It's time for all good little girls to be in bed." He led her out his door and to her own. "Go inside," he ordered, "before I forget I'm an honorable man."

Her gaze flew to his. The moonlight streaming through the window at the end of the hallway illuminated his strong features, outlined his shoulders against the darker shadows behind them. "That isn't possible," she whispered, filled with longing so intense she ached. "Honor comes from the inner self. It can't be put aside."

"Even wise men can be tempted beyond control. I don't intend to let things get that far." His quiet laugh was sardonic and directed at himself.

"You use coldness to put distance between yourself and others," she told him, "but that isn't you. You deny yourself the very things you want because you were hurt in the past by those you let get too close. Your parents, I think, and maybe others."

He turned his face from her. In the moonlight, his profile was like that of a sculpture, remote and unfeeling, a beautiful carving of stone.

"Go to bed, rich girl," he ordered. "Maybe in your dreams you'll find Prince Charming." He turned away and nearly disappeared in the dark. Only the fact that he was moving, heading for his door, gave his presence away.

"I always thought the Beast was the more interesting character in the fairy tales," she called softly after him, managing to put laughter into the retort.

Climbing into bed a short time later, she felt the odd sadness descend on her again. She prayed for her nephew, for Matthew and Claudia, and for their dark knight, sent to save them from evil. But who was going to save him?

"The missing cowboy is our link," Dev said.

He sat in the sheriff's office, going over the evidence once more with Grayhawk. He had taken the fingerprints of everyone at the ranch house, either directly while he questioned them, or subtly by lifting them from a glass.

"Maybe. But no one matched the fingerprint found at the hotel," Wyatt said. "Nor did any of those we dusted at the bunkhouse right after the kidnapping."

"That doesn't prove it wasn't the cowboy."

"Doesn't prove it was, either," Wyatt pointed out.

He picked up the telephone when it rang. "Oh, hi, Hub. How's it going? Yeah? Interesting."

Dev muttered an expletive. In any other case, if the family involved wasn't as rich and well-known as the Fortunes, he would have filed a report and put the case on the back burner. His boss hadn't once asked him to wrap it up and get on something else.

He rubbed his eyes. Staying up all day and half or more of each night, watching the comings and goings of everyone at the main ranch quarters, was wearing him down.

August sixth to August fifteenth. Nine days. That wasn't so very long on a case. But it felt longer.

Because of Vanessa?

His body tightened. She certainly contributed to the sleepless nights. Lordy, but he wanted her...dreamed of her...fantasized about her... It was a wonder the zippers were still intact on any of his pants. He stayed hard nearly all the time.

A physical reaction. That's all it was, no matter how she tried to pretend otherwise. No meeting of the souls. No stars spinning out of orbit. No emotional involvement, other than that caused by the tragedy of events that had brought them together. He felt sorry for her, for her whole family. No one deserved this kind of grief.

And no child deserved the kind of fear that went with being uprooted from a secure world and thrust into the unknown.

"Hell," Wyatt said upon slamming down the telephone.

Dev observed the sheriff's disgusted grimace. "What?"

"That was Hubcap Johnson. He just confessed to the kidnapping."

"A chronic confessor?"

"Yeah, only this time he knew—"

Dev frowned impatiently when Wyatt paused as if hating to add the rest.

"He knew about the words cut from the newspapers."

A chill blasted Dev's neck. The hair stood up. "Several people saw the note."

"He said he cut the words from the *Leather Bucket Weekly*…back in April, about the first week of the month, he thought."

"So much for our confidential information," Dev muttered. "Who else knew besides Vanessa?"

Wyatt counted the numbers up. "The deputy working on the case, his partner. The young deputy whose girlfriend told him about the strange cuts on the table at the motel. She might have known the date of the damage since her father owns the place. You. Me. That's it."

"And Vanessa."

"She knows the rules. She wouldn't tell anyone," Wyatt assured him in a cool tone.

"Yeah, only everyone she knows and trusts."

He stalked out of the lawman's office three hours later, his fury not abated one bit. He'd noted the sheriff's reactive manner when he'd added Vanessa's name to the list of those who knew about the date on the ransom note.

Grayhawk had had the old man brought in for questioning. Dev had grilled him intensely on how he came by his insider information. The old codger was crazy as a loon and crafty as only the old and wary can be. They hadn't gotten a thing out of him. But he had said something about the girl telling him.

Was that girl Vanessa?

Had she—in confidence, of course—told a friend about the clue they had happened upon? He gritted his teeth. He would soon find out.

At the ranch, he parked in his usual spot in the shade, which everyone now left for him, and headed into the house.

After searching through room after room, he stopped in frustration. With the place usually teeming with people, why the hell couldn't he find a single person who could tell him where she was?

He drove the half mile to the stables.

That's where he found her. Cruz leaned on the gate outside a large arena. Vanessa, as strong and supple as a willow stick, sat astride a big black horse. The ring was set with hurdles and walls made from haystacks. She and the horse were taking them at a fast clip. Too fast, he thought, but he was no expert.

Horse and rider flowed as one, a single ripple sailing down a clear stream. She spoke softly. The horse shook his head as if refusing a request. Dev heard her speak again. He realized that she was having trouble.

The horse balked at a jump, rearing into the air and shaking his head as if throwing off flies. The rider leaned forward. Only her feet in the stirrups kept her on the animal. Beside him, Cruz cursed the horse, but made no move to intervene.

"Is she in danger?" Dev asked, his heart squeezed down to the size of a walnut.

Cruz shrugged.

"Dammit, is she in danger?"

"She's in control."

Dev swore in frustration. "If she gets hurt, I'll shoot the horse, then you," he heard himself say.

For a moment he had the oddest sensation—as if he were above the scene, watching the horse and rider, the trainer who didn't seem concerned, himself as he fought the need to rush into the arena and get her off the animal.

Yeah, Kincaid to the rescue, he mocked the need as the sensation passed. He was suspended in that confusing state that came from having had a dream so vivid he couldn't quite tell if it had been fiction or real.

The horse trumpeted, rising in the air and shaking his head again, seizing control from the human who clung so doggedly to his back.

"That horse is wild," Dev said, an accusation.

Cruz turned a cool glance on him, then studied the pair in the ring again. "His dam was wild, part mustang, part Thoroughbred. I bought him at auction in Arizona. Everyone was afraid of his temper. Stallions can be unpredictable."

"You put her on a wild stallion?" Murder came to Dev's mind as the trainer turned back to the ring.

The horse leaped forward in an all-out run when he brought all four hooves back to the ground. He swerved at the fence, then raced around it. Dev saw that Vanessa was urging him on with swishing strokes of a riding crop along his flanks.

"Watch," Cruz advised. He climbed on the top rail. The horse ran and ran. When he slowed, Vanessa pushed him on. Finally, the horse showed his teeth. He dropped his head and made a few snapping motions. Then, sides heaving, he stopped.

She slipped off him, her body slender, flexible, confident. Leaving the reins tied over his back, she waved the crop at the horse. He ran, then fell into a trot. Finishing the circuit of the ring, he stopped again.

Dev observed, puzzled, as Vanessa turned her back on her mount and walked toward the center of the ring. She plucked at one of the hay bales, keeping her back to the stallion. He walked a few steps toward her.

She laid the quirt on the bale and dug something out of her pocket. The horse snuffled at her neck. She hunched her shoulder and turned away again. The horse nudged her back a couple of times. Finally she turned to the stallion.

A knot formed in Dev's throat at how tiny she appeared next to the stallion. She talked quietly and gently stroked the shiny length of the stallion's neck. The horse dipped his head as if agreeing.

She gave the horse a tidbit to eat. Then she climbed into the saddle once more.

This time the stallion behaved much better. He let her set the pace. He took each hurdle straight-on with no balking, no prancing and no angling into them. They made the round without mishap.

Her face was shining when she rode past them toward the barn. "Isn't he a beaut? He's going to be great, Cruz."

"Right." Perez shoved his hat back off his forehead when horse and rider rode on. "She's good," he said in a satisfied tone. "Almost as good as me."

Dev considered coldcocking the man, but thought better of it. He would be taking his anger out on the wrong person. He strode to his vehicle and returned to the house.

Going to the breakfast room where coffee, tea and snacks were available at nearly any hour of the day, he poured a glass of tea and drank it down. It didn't cool his temper. He went to his room and took a shower.

When he finished, he could hear the water running next door. He pictured the room, which backed up to his. From there it was only a jump to other images, those of her naked and wet, hair streaming around her shoulders in wild disarray, eyes daring him to reach out and take what she so boldly offered.

In a rare loss of control, he banged his fist against the adjoining wall. The water stopped abruptly.

He dressed then paced the length of the room. He'd give her ten minutes to dress, then they were going to have a long, serious talk.

Vanessa listened, but didn't hear anything else. She worried about the mysterious thump in Dev's room. Had he fallen? Maybe hit his head? Was he lying on the floor, bleeding?

She wrapped a towel around her hair turban-style and pulled on a thigh-length terry robe. Going to the door between their rooms, she listened again, then knocked.

"Dev? Are you okay?"

From the other room, she heard the slide of metal

against metal, then the door opened. Dev glared at her.

"I heard something. Did you fall?"

"No," he said.

Hmm, he was definitely snarling. "Is something wrong?"

"Yes. Everything and then some. Why wasn't this door locked?" His glare was enough to melt rock.

"It was. You—"

"I don't mean on my side. Why wasn't it locked on yours?"

She gave him a wicked grin. "What for? I never intended to lock you out. You're the one who wants distance."

"I need to talk to you." He stepped into her room, backed her into a chair, then stood over her. "Who did you tell about the ransom note?"

She looked at him blankly.

"The date we found," he snapped. "And that the clippings came from the *Leather Bucket Weekly*."

"No one."

He raked a hand through his hair. She noted that it was damp. The scent of his talc and shaving lotion drifted around her. She inhaled it like a starving man at a feast.

"Don't give me that. The sheriff just had a confession from some old man who knew that the note had been cut from the *Leather Bucket Weekly* during the early part of April. You must have mentioned the facts to one of your girlfriends recently...over a friendly lunch, perhaps?"

She shook her head. The towel loosened and she tucked the end in more securely.

"Look, I know you didn't mean to, that it slipped out—"

"No, it didn't," she spoke up, angrier than she'd ever been with him. "That was probably Hubcap Johnson. He confesses to every crime he hears about."

"Yeah, but this time he had facts. He said he overheard some girl mention the ransom note."

"And of course you thought it had to be me." She stood, returning glare for glare, their noses no more than six inches apart. "It could have been the deputy's girlfriend. After all, her father owns the motel. She knew about the kidnapping, the date the furniture was damaged, that you checked the place for fingerprints, the whole bit. It could have been the maid who cleans the room. It could have been the owner's wife or girlfriend. It could have been anyone!" She lowered her voice. "But it wasn't me. You got that?"

An eternity went by, then another.

"You swear you haven't mentioned it to a soul?" He gave her one of his narrow-eyed stares.

"Yes."

"All right."

"All right? Just like that?"

"Yes."

"Huh."

He grinned at her indignant huff. It was so engaging, she became flustered. Dropping her gaze from his, she saw he was barefoot. A smile popped out of her anger, frustration, yearning, and all the other emotions he engendered in her.

"It seems odd to be grilled by a barefoot FBI

agent,'' she murmured, giving him a teasing, oblique glance.

He glanced down at his feet, then at hers. Slowly his gaze wound its way along her legs, to her thighs and the robe that had gaped so that nearly all her thigh was visible. Her breath shortened as he paused, then moved ever so slowly along her body, stopping again at the deep vee of bare skin visible at the neckline of the robe.

Suddenly self-conscious at her skimpy apparel, she crossed the lapels more securely and tightened the sash.

"No," he said.

A frisson rushed along her nerves. His voice was deep, husky, vibrant, alluring, sexy.

His gaze darkened, became slumberous, hot, hungry, moody.

She had to open her mouth and gasp at what air she could force into her lungs. Her legs felt as if they would collapse at any moment.

He reached out and caught a strand of hair that had escaped the towel. He fingered it, then reached up and slowly pushed the towel to the back. It fell with a soft plop. She felt the quick rush of air as it hit the floor behind her.

Then all was still.

He closed his hand in her hair, taking a fistful as if it were precious gems he had discovered.

"I've wondered how this would look spread out over my pillow every night from the first...from the first moment we met."

"Yes."

His voice sank to a deeper, rougher level. "You're

a temptation no mortal man can be expected to resist forever.''

"Yes."

"I've never had this problem before."

She was silent, letting him sort it out.

"Why, dammit?"

She waited.

"Why?" He sounded angry, perplexed.

"Because," she whispered, the yearning breaking through to unbearable longing. She would die if he didn't kiss her.

"Yes, because," he agreed, a smile barely tucking up the corners of his perfectly chiseled mouth, the touch of amusement acknowledging the futility of fighting the attraction a moment longer.

Everything in her tightened—her breasts and nipples, someplace deep within her body, her soul.

This time she wasn't the one who took the necessary step to bring them together. He did it. He slipped one bare foot between hers, and his arms gathered her close.

Heaven. It was heaven.

She laid her hands on his waist, needing support as his lips ravaged her face in gentle forays. She turned her lips to his, but he evaded her, moving instead to the side of her neck, then drifting down the line of terry cloth to the point where the material met.

Her breath hung in her throat while her heart looped and circled and plunged like a kite.

"This isn't going anywhere," he muttered.

"No," she agreed hazily, sliding her hands under the soft cotton and onto his skin. Oh, bliss… "I've wanted to touch you for so long."

"I know." He dragged his mouth upward, flitted by her lips and nuzzled her temple. "It was in your eyes. Every day. Every night. You drove me crazy."

"That's fair. You drove me crazy, too."

"I've never wanted like this. It's…painful."

"Yes."

He lifted his head and gave her a long, questioning perusal. "I wonder if you know."

"I know what it is to want." She slid her hands over his back, loving the warm feel of him, the latent strength she sensed in the broad expanse of flesh. He was only an inch or so taller than the men in her family, but he seemed much larger to her. He filled her whole horizon.

And her heart.

A cynical glitter appeared in his eyes. "Yeah, right. You have only to reach and whatever you want is in your grasp."

"Not always. Life hasn't always been that easy."

"Huh."

She smiled at his usual snort of disbelief. The smile fled when he moved even closer. She opened her legs and embraced him with her thighs. The robe shifted and fell aside. His thigh pressed intimately against her.

A gasp of pure need escaped her. She caught her bottom lip between her teeth and stared at him, at the intimacy between them. Dizziness washed through her.

He caught the belt on each side and slowly the knot slipped apart, then fell away to dangle at her sides. The robe shifted, then hung in a straight line down her body, the lapels barely touching at the exact center.

"Nothing is going to happen," he said.

"How do you know?"

"I'm not going to let it."

She wasn't sure they could stop.

He bent and placed one kiss in the indentation between her breasts. She breathed deeply, lifting toward him.

"You want more?"

"Yes."

"This?"

He slipped his hands inside the robe and clasped her waist while his mouth roamed over the further exposed flesh. The robe clung to the fullness of her breasts, barely hiding the erect nipples.

"This?"

With the gentlest of love bites, he moved downward until his lips touched the spot just above her breast. Then he pushed the material aside.

She nearly fainted when he enclosed her in his mouth and rubbed his tongue over the sensitive tip. Never had she known such bliss. "Never," she whispered.

Caught in a passion she hadn't previously experienced, she reacted instinctively, rubbing and moving against him, feeling as sinuous as a cat.

She was passion-flushed now. Heat throbbed in every part of her. She wanted the robe off. She wanted skin on skin. "The bed," she murmured, needing to lie down, feeling she would fall if she didn't.

"No bed," he growled. He moved to her other

breast and repeated all the wonderful things he had just done.

"I'm going to fall," she warned, and grabbed his waist, hooking her thumbs in the waistband of his jeans. She found they weren't snapped. It was an easy job to slide the zipper down and discover he wore no briefs.

He raised his head, saw the easy chair and in one smooth motion settled into it with her on his lap. Then his mouth was on hers, delighting, demanding, taking, giving.

Her hands were captured and held against his chest. "Please," she murmured. "I need...to touch you."

"No. If we go further...no, we can't..."

"Why not? Take your shirt off."

He let her tug his shirt up, then he helped her push it over his head and out of the way. He groaned when she leaned into him. Her breasts swelled and engorged, feeding on the heat generated by their bodies.

"It would be too good." He enclosed her in a tight embrace, trapping her hands between them.

She opened her eyes and stared at him, perplexed.

"Much too good. We're ready to explode right now. Just touching...here." He slipped a hand between them and took her breast into his palm.

He kneaded each breast, then slid his hand down onto her thigh. She gasped and held her breath.

"You want more. You want all the touching, all the kissing, all that comes after that. And it would be so damn good...to be in you, all the way..."

"Mmm," she said impatiently.

"But that could cause problems..."

"No." She touched his cheek, ran her fingers down

his throat, through his hair, over his shoulders. Touching him, just touching him. For the moment, it was enough.

"I'm on a case. You're involved—"

"How?" She sat up, startled.

He shook his head. "Not with the kidnappers. It's... You're the daughter of the house, a very rich house. I'll be moving on in a few days, a week or two at the most."

His eyes were oceans deep, mysterious and darkly compelling. The call of something fierce and wild and forever drummed in her breast.

"Just for tonight, let me look at you. We won't go all the way, but for tonight...just this far."

He slipped the robe off her shoulders and tossed it aside, then he smoothed the tangles of damp hair around her face, laying the strands over her breasts, then pushing them to her back as if he couldn't bear to have that view obstructed.

"You're the most beautiful woman I've ever met," he said in a low, hoarse voice.

His fingers trailed over her breasts, down her side, over her hip. He caressed her leg to her knee and back.

"There are a thousand things I'd like to do to you."

"Then do them," she offered simply.

"No. That's too dangerous."

He pulled her back into his arms and slowly—so slowly she thought she would die—he kissed her. And it was everything she'd dreamed bliss would be. They explored each other thoroughly.

"If we stop here, there'll be no regrets," he murmured eons later. "If we stop now."

Six

"If you stop now, I'll never forgive you."

Dev knew they had reached the point of no return. He was past caring. His conscience had burned up long ago in the hot passion they shared, sometime between when she had explored his body as thoroughly as possible after he'd shucked his jeans and this moment when he'd at last allowed himself to touch the soft, dewy petals of her womanhood.

He rose with her in his arms and carried her to the queen-size bed, which was already turned down, and laid her on the sheet. He stood there, giving her a chance to back down, to tell him to get out of her room.

She smiled up at him, all the promises of springtime in her green eyes. He gritted his teeth as a yearning for all the things he'd missed and longed for all the days of his life spiraled through him.

Were the promises real?

He shook his head slightly. Damned if he knew.

"This is…" he muttered. "This is real."

"Yes," she murmured, moving over to give him room.

He carefully lay beside her and propped himself up on an elbow. He slid his leg over hers, not to hold her—or maybe that was the primitive urge behind the act—but he wanted to feel her, too. He wanted skin against skin, the tactile sensation of her flesh on his.

"You're real. And yet you're a dream."

"So are you." She shifted so that she could sandwich their thighs together, and ran one hand over his chest.

"Every man's dream," he continued, "that ever saw you."

Her grin was quick, surprising, amused. "But only one man's reality. Yours. As you are mine."

He kissed her again, taking all the wonder of her into himself until his head spun with desires he could no longer control. She was his. For tonight.

And then that thought, too, disappeared into stardust as she touched him intimately. He groaned and made himself take it slow when he wanted only to sink into her and give way to the hunger…and yet, he wanted it to last.

Contradictions. His life had been filled with contradictions from the moment they had met.

He kissed each perfectly formed breast again, then moved slowly down her body. She watched him with curiosity in her eyes and a tender smile on her face. He gazed into her eyes for a long ten seconds, then dipped his head and slid lower.

"Oh," she said on a gasp.

Eyes closed, the blood humming through him with the muted roar of a high-speed train, he tasted the sweetness of her flesh, felt the throb of desire in her, the welcome in her body. Her whimpers of passion and the feel of her fingers in his hair filled him with a primitive joy that made him want to shout.

But not yet. First there was this.

"Dev, oh, darling, please, I'm going to…to… Please. Come to me. Now."

Her wild hunger drove his own. He rose and lifted himself away from her.

"No, don't go." She reached for him.

"I'm not leaving." He couldn't have left if the devil himself appeared and told him his soul was in peril if he stayed another second. He went to his room and returned in less than a minute. She saw what he had done and nodded solemnly as if praising him for thinking of protection.

"Now," he said.

He covered her slender nakedness with his body. Slowly, carefully, while she watched, her eyes slumberous yet bright with interest, he fitted them together in the way nature intended. When he was as far as he could go, he released the breath he'd been holding.

"It's okay. It doesn't hurt," she assured him. She gave him a radiant smile. "It's a tight fit, but…it's okay. Wonderful, actually."

He had to laugh at her enthusiasm. She was as open and uninhibited as a child in her delight with everything they did. For some reason that touched something within him that had been wary and uncertain. Now it was okay. She had said so. He relaxed…as much as a man who was on the brink of coming apart at the seams could.

"Wonderful," he murmured.

He began to move in her, knowing he wouldn't last long if she didn't stay still. She didn't. She moved in rhythm with him, rising and falling in sync, a perfect duet…

With her, he found that making love could be part

of the fantasy of life, composed of dreams and reality in equal parts. It was more than anything he'd ever experienced, more than he'd ever longed for or dreamed of.

She arched against him and cried out in a low, keening tone. Her breath stopped. He continued stroking her with his hand, but paused in the mind-boggling thrusts for a moment.

"No," she protested. "Move with me. Now."

Taking a breath, he let himself plunge over the edge into the torrent of pure passion. It filled his mind like a flash flood through a narrow canyon, washing all before it but the sound and sensation of fulfillment, complete and without mercy.

It was minutes before he could move again. When he rolled onto his side, she turned with him, holding them together in the intimate embrace.

She used the sheet to gently wipe the perspiration from his face, then hers. The green eyes were hazy and warm as she watched him.

A question that had flitted through his mind then disappeared in the heat of their joining, came to him. This was a situation he'd never met before. He wasn't sure if he should ask. She saved him the bother.

"I knew it would be like this—wild and sweet and heart-stopping…and the afterglow… It's the deepest peace I've ever known. A gift to men and women for living. Wasn't it wonderful?" She sounded so pleased with it all. As if they, instead of Adam and Eve, had discovered sex.

Laughing softly, she leaned over and kissed him, an endearing pressing of her lips to his that seemed as innocent as a baby's touch.

He tried to ignore the thought that kept intruding. Finally he had to make sure. "Was this…this wasn't the…this couldn't have been your first time."

She kissed the middle of his chest, then started working her way to his nipple. He curved a finger under her chin and made her look at him.

"Was it?"

"Of course."

"Why?"

One of her solemn expressions appeared. "Because it was the right time. Because you're the right man. Because."

Her slight shrug expressed a helplessness that he understood. Some things were more powerful than mere mortals could comprehend. Sex—no—not sex, but the attraction they felt for each other, was one of those.

He had never before encountered any woman he couldn't walk away from. What had happened just now scared him. It was beyond his understanding—

"We had better dress. It's nearly time for dinner."

"Oh, God," he groaned. "I have to face your father."

She laughed out loud. "Well, yes, but we don't have to confess like a couple of kids who stole a strawberry pie, do we?" She told him about the time two of her brothers had done that. "Father wouldn't let any of us eat dinner until the culprits confessed. We just sat and waited. After fifteen minutes, they couldn't stand it, so they told all."

He swung out of bed, surprised and angry with himself when he realized he didn't want to leave her. Not yet. He hadn't had near enough…

With a silent curse, he gathered his scattered clothing and stalked out of her room. He showered again. So did she. When he stepped out into the courtyard, she joined him.

He was aware of her, of her scent, of the cool green silk outfit she wore, of the hot satin of her skin, of her brightness, as sparkling as a new penny, and her sweet warmth, on the way to where her family waited—her father, Lily, Matthew, Claudia, her two brothers, her aunt Mary Ellen, Logan, Mary Ellen's younger son, and Clint Lockhart, Mary Ellen's brother.

When he had questioned Mary Ellen's side of the family, Dev had liked her openness. The two men had been more difficult to read. The son was impatient as were all the Fortunes. The brother had been full of helpful advice, volunteering more information than was asked, but there was an undercurrent of surliness about the man.

As they approached the others gathered in the shade of the trellis for before-dinner drinks, Dev felt as if every pair of eyes was looking right inside him…and could see every caress of that wild romp between him and the daughter of the house.

Heat slithered into the back of his neck. He hoped his ears weren't red. He wondered how long they would have to sit before he broke down and confessed all to her father, who watched him with a narrowed gaze and more than a hint of—suspicion?—in his dark eyes.

Dev swallowed hard. He had never let anything interfere in an investigation, had never let passion come between him and the job to be done. He'd never slept with a redheaded, green-eyed virgin, either, one who had turned him inside out and upside down before their tryst had ended.

A jolt of lightning ran through him. He didn't know if it was delight or despair. A hell of a mess he'd gotten himself into.

Vanessa faced her family with self-enforced calm. She accepted her usual champagne from her brother and chose a seat a little apart from the others. She needed to be alone for a while to mull over this new knowledge of the male-female relationship.

In making love with Dev, she had expected the excitement. But the closeness...that was something new. And the deep peace she'd felt in her soul in the afterglow.

She wanted to hug it to herself, keep her secret—hers and Dev's—and not share it with anyone else. Not yet. It was too new, too fragile, too perfect.

Glancing at her family, she observed her father and Lily, seated beside each other. She wanted her love to be close to her. She wanted to be free to touch him and feel his presence nearby.

Seeing her father watching her in a pensive manner, she dredged up a smile for him. She now understood why couples went on honeymoons. They needed this special time for each other, to bond—

"I don't suppose you have anything new?" Matthew asked.

His face was so grim Vanessa felt a deep pain in her heart for him. His life wasn't working out. She didn't know if he and Claudia would make it. She wondered if she should probe a bit to see if she could help.

Maybe she should talk to Claudia. Her sister-in-law had problems with the family name and wealth. However, she needed to find the confidence in Matthew's love within herself. No one could give it to her. Sighing, Vanessa turned to Dev.

He hesitated, his gaze surveying the group before he spoke. "As a matter of fact, I do have information. The detective has a lead on the cowboy who was here."

Vanessa watched him observe the reactions of her family to this news. She, too, glanced around the group. They were all staring at Dev with varying expressions—some with hope and anxiety, some with doubt that this was helpful news, and some with anger in their faces.

Clint waved his hand in disdain. "I don't see how that will help. He certainly didn't leave with any baby. I saw him take off in his truck."

"He can verify your location at the time of the kidnapping," Dev remarked in that polite way he had, which gave nothing away.

Anger erupted as Clint stiffened and glared at the agent. "Are you doubting my word?" he asked with a dangerous edge.

Dev wasn't intimidated. "I like to tie up loose ends," he said smoothly.

Vanessa relaxed. Dev had everything under control. Catching Lily's gaze on her, she felt heat slide into her face. There was something in the older woman's eyes that spoke of understanding. There was tenderness in her expression. Vanessa was suddenly sure her future stepmother knew about her involvement with Dev.

Lily smiled, glanced at Dev, then nodded.

Vanessa, bathed in the warm glow of the other woman's approval, smiled, too. At that moment her aunt, seated to her left, laid a hand on her arm and squeezed. Vanessa saw kindness in the gaze Aunt Mary Ellen turned on her.

Her heart swelled, filling her with so much love she felt it would burst out of her, showering all her family in the richness of her feelings.

She wanted so much for each of them—for Matthew and Claudia to get their son back and find the happiness they deserved, for her aunt to find someone who would be true and love her with all his heart, for her father and Lily to be able to marry and share their love freely—

"It's time to go in," her father announced. He stood and held his arm out toward her.

Surprised, Vanessa joined him as they headed for the dining room. Uncle Clint bowed, then gallantly escorted Lily while Logan did the honors for his mother. Matthew, Claudia, and the rest followed.

"Dev, won't you join us at this end of the table?" her father requested.

The next thing she knew she was seated to her father's right with Dev beside her. Lily sat on the left side of the table. Vanessa didn't miss the scowl that flashed through Uncle Clint's eyes at the arrangement. She wondered what his problem was. But then he'd always been a person given to dark moods.

Glancing at Dev, she saw his deep blue gaze take in the scowl, then pass swiftly around the table. She wondered what he thought as he scrutinized her family with eyes that seemed to see all. He turned his head and looked directly at her at that moment.

Pleasure speared through her, painful in its intensity. She couldn't wait until they were alone again. She wanted to explore this new experience with him again and again until she understood all the many nuances of making love.

The meal seemed to take forever, but at last they finished.

"Excuse me," she said as soon as they adjourned to the great room for coffee. "I think I'll go now. Good night, all." She kissed her aunt and father, then crossed the courtyard to her room, aware of several pairs of eyes on her back. Her heart dipped and reeled like a drunken butterfly.

Restless, she waited for Dev to return. It was more than two hours. When she heard the outer door open and close, she rushed to the connecting doorway.

Dev stopped inside the room and gazed at her, his eyes troubled by thoughts she couldn't read. Some of the joy evaporated. He wasn't thrilled to be alone with her.

"What?" she asked softly.

He sighed and tugged off his tie, then tossed it and his jacket to a chair. He crossed the room and stood in front of her. "I think we need to lock this again."

"Why?"

"You know why."

She crossed her arms, holding in the emotions that threatened to spill over. "No. Tell me."

"It isn't right—"

"It wasn't wrong," she interrupted. "What we did wasn't wrong. How can you say it was?"

Dev didn't look at her. He couldn't. She was too beautiful, too tempting…too fragile in her unwanted feelings for him. Damn, he'd never asked for this!

"Because," he said carefully, "you're the daughter of the house. I'm…" He didn't know how to describe himself. "A temporary fixture in your life. I go where the FBI sends me."

"Doesn't the FBI allow you to have anyone else in your life? Is it all work and nothing else?"

"Mostly," he agreed, keeping the edge off with an effort. "I should never have touched you."

Pain rippled across her face, but she didn't look away. "It's too late for regrets."

"Don't you think I know that?" He spun from the temptation of her. She was fresh and sweet and brave. And he wanted her more than life itself. But… "There are too many differences. My time here is almost up."

She looked startled. "Are you about to solve the case?"

"No. I only meant that I'll probably be sent elsewhere soon if we don't get a break here."

"You'll leave alone, and you won't return." She faced his sharp glance with a level stare that spoke of her honesty.

"Look, you're on a thrill kick, sleeping with an FBI agent. I'm different from your usual friends." He saw no future for them and no point in dragging things out. "Your father is aware of the electricity between us. He doesn't approve."

Her eyes flashed dangerously. "He said that?"

"Of course not. He didn't have to. I can read between the lines." Her father would probably have his hide stripped and then tie him to an anthill.

"He sat us next to each other tonight," she reminded him, her chin at its usual stubborn angle.

Dev saw there was no use in arguing with her. She came from a privileged life and was used to having her own way. She thought she wanted him. That was reason enough in her viewpoint to have him.

"He would probably gift wrap and hand me over if he thought that would make you happy. It won't."

She thought what they had shared was the promise of more good things to come, but he knew about promises. Hadn't he seen the despair in his mother's eyes each time his father broke his vow to never hurt them again? Hadn't he seen the same despair in his partner's widow? Stan had often assured her he wouldn't get killed.

Promises, Dev had learned at an early age, could not be trusted. His job was dangerous and he wouldn't make promises to anyone, especially *her* with her glowing belief in life.

"It would. We're right together. We proved it earlier today." Her smile was gentle, teasing.

He had to wipe the foolishness out of her. It was better to hurt a little now than a lot later on. There was no hope for them, and one of them had to be practical about it. "We had great sex. That's all."

She shook her head, her eyes going solemn, vulnerable in the way that made him ache to hold her and tell her all would be fine. He struggled against the pull and allure of her, the golden web of need she wove around him.

"That's all it can be," he muttered doggedly.

"Tell me about your family," she invited.

He frowned as he considered the request, which made no sense. "Why?"

"To help me understand why you're shutting me out."

"Do you think that once a man has you, he won't be able to resist you?"

"Not any man," she said calmly. "Just you."

Her words were so close to the truth he'd suspected while they were making love, it scared him. He had to crush the hunger between them.

"You're a good roll in the hay, but I've had better." He yawned and stepped back, taking hold of the door and starting to close it. "Now, I need some sleep. I have a lot of ground to cover tomorrow. I'll be staying in town for a couple of days."

She stepped back into her room without another word when he closed the door. He resented the quiet dignity of her acceptance. It would have been easier if she'd shouted or cried or done something to prove he was right.

When the latch snapped into place, he slid the bolt home, locking her out. Then he stood there in the dark, the glow that came from her, gone now. He wished… For a moment, he wished he believed in promises.

Dev stared grumpily at Sam Waterman who had taken over ranch security after the kidnapping. "No further information from McCoy?"

The private detective pushed his plate aside. They were at a sidewalk café in San Antonio. The noise of other diners and tourists enjoying the riverwalk kept their voices from carrying far.

"None. The cowboy hasn't shown up at any of his usual haunts, including a shoestring ranch he's trying to run out near Amarillo."

"It's a strange case, this cat and mouse game."

"Sometimes I think it's more about hurting the family than about money," Sam said. His frown was fierce. "But to take a kid this way...I don't know. The whole thing feels wacky."

"I agree." Dev smiled grimly when the older man gave him a quick glance. "There's more going on than meets the eye. There's tension between several members of the Fortune family. I can't quite figure out how it all connects."

"But you think it does," Sam concluded. He glanced at his watch. "I have to go. You think we need to put some men at the ranch again? Ryan said you FBI honchos didn't want anyone mucking about."

"No. There's been no sign of further danger. Thanks for the information." He picked up a sealed envelope and put it in his inside pocket.

"Any time. See you."

Dev watched the other man leave. He and Sam had been in a couple of tight spots together. He trusted him as much as he allowed himself to trust any other person.

"Hello," a female voice said, breaking into his reverie. Without turning, he knew she was pretty and sexy and well aware of both those facts. He faced the woman, knowing who she was by some instinct that came from his years of observing people.

She took his notice as an invitation to join him. "I'm Sophia Fortune. We haven't met, but I know Sam. When I saw you together, I assumed you were the FBI agent on the case."

Her Texas drawl was soft and disarming. There was a question in her last statement.

She was as he'd surmised—pretty, sexy and confident. The wicked stepmother—Vanessa's view of the woman—was a well-built strawberry-blonde in a pink silk sheath. Big blue eyes. Pouty smile. Good legs. She looked like a woman who had a lot of things on her mind, most of them unspeakable in polite society.

Her age was hard to determine on looks alone. She took care of herself and knew how to enhance her best features. He knew her to be thirty-nine. He'd read the sheriff's report on her and her airtight alibi during the kidnapping. He also knew Sam had a man watching her.

"Special Agent Devin Kincaid," he told her.

"You're working on the kidnapping?"

"That's right." He wondered how much she knew. He raised his eyebrows in question.

"I know this might sound strange, considering Ryan and I are in the middle of a divorce, but I'm worried about the baby. I guess women always have a soft spot when it comes to children." Her expression of concern seemed genuine. She looked at him as if she were entitled to a full on-the-spot report.

"Yeah, Baby, uh…" He pretended to search for the name.

"The Fortune baby," she prompted.

"Baby Bryan. Your grandchild," he added softly. "Until the divorce."

A pale flush enhanced the color on her cheeks. Anger, he wondered, or feelings for the child as she'd implied?

"I don't know him," she explained with a helpless shrug. "He was born after my husband and I broke up. But he's so young, well, I was naturally concerned."

"Of course. Unfortunately, there's no news."

"This must be tearing the family apart. Matthew and Claudia…well, it's no secret they're having problems. The Fortune family can be difficult for outsiders to deal with. They're a law unto themselves." Again the helpless shrug and a glance that included him with the group of outsiders.

"Does Sam still have detectives all over the place?" she asked with an edge of sardonic amusement.

"Not since I was brought in."

She gave him a sweetly sympathetic smile. "Ryan is probably furious that you haven't solved the case yet. He can be…impatient."

This last was said in delicate tones, as if she hated to mention this one tiny but fatal flaw of the Fortune patriarch. Dev grinned. "That could safely be said of most of the family."

Sophia smiled and touched his arm companionably, just the tips of fingers, then she withdrew. "I'm sure you've observed that often in the two weeks you've been there. They expect their wishes to be carried out at once."

"Hmm," he said.

She took that for agreement. "I tried hard enough to please the whole clan, but it was wasted effort. I never felt part of them. I suppose I wasn't good enough. I was a nurse, you see, before my marriage. Some of us had to work for a living."

In making a bid for pity, he had to admit she was good. Her sorrow looked convincing. Maybe it was. Maybe she regretted losing her hold on the goose that laid all those nice golden eggs for her—the town house in Austin where she entertained politicians and rock stars and the younger men she seemed to prefer as lovers, the jewels, the expensive cars and other perks that came with money.

Sophia Fortune had overplayed her hand with her much older husband. She'd lost. However, she wasn't a woman to give in gracefully, according to Sam, Wyatt, and Vanessa, all of whom were old friends and insiders. He was as much an outsider as Sophia portrayed herself to be.

At the thought of Vanessa, his insides tightened painfully. Less than forty-eight hours away from the ranch and all he thought about was getting back. Not a good thing.

"I must run," his guest told him, her eyes big with regret. "Please, call me if you hear anything. I really am concerned." She handed him a card.

"I will," he promised. He glanced at the card, which contained her address and phone number, and stored it in his inner pocket along with the information Sam had collected for him. He stood politely when she did.

Tears filled her eyes. "I've heard that few children

are recovered alive after the first twenty-four hours. It's so sad."

He didn't move when she stepped forward, then leaned against him as if overcome with grief. He handed her a napkin and moved to the side.

She recovered her poise. "I must go."

He waited until she finished her farewells and left, then sat when she was out of sight and sipped the fresh coffee the waiter had brought while they had talked.

"Interesting," he murmured after a long, thoughtful period of mulling over their conversation. The woman had wanted information. She'd used all her charm to that end.

When she'd pressed her card into his hand, there had been an invitation in her eyes. Her allure was all surface sparkle and flash, though.

A picture of Vanessa sprang to mind. Her freshness. Her lack of guile. Her surety that they were meant for each other. That would last about two months, he figured. Then she'd grow tired of the novelty and return to her rich friends. Where she belonged.

Seven

Vanessa hung up the phone and paced from window to window in her room. Sunday had come and gone. It was now late Monday afternoon and Dev still hadn't returned.

Two friends had called to say they had seen him in San Antonio at one of the riverwalk cafés. With Sophia.

An unrealistic sense of betrayal beat through her blood. She had no right to feel that way. He'd never promised her anything.

She swallowed hard against the tears that clogged her throat. What was it within her that always expected things to turn out wonderful? It was time she learned differently.

Her grandfather, her mother, Uncle Cameron—life had changed with each death. Sophia had snagged her father and life had become more difficult with each passing year. Matthew had found his true love, only that wasn't working, either. Her father's divorce, the kidnapping, all contributed to a sense of foreboding about her family's future. The ranch, always a safe haven, had been invaded.

And then there was Devin Kincaid, their shining knight with the tortured eyes, sent to find the baby and restore order in their disarrayed lives.

But he didn't want to be involved in their messy problems. He wanted to do the job and leave. Who could blame him? She sometimes wanted to walk away, too.

But she couldn't. This was her family, the only one she was likely to have. The tears pressed closer. She pushed them back. She would not cry. She wouldn't.

A shadow moved across the window, startling her. The rapid tattoo of her heart told her who it was before she heard the door open and close in the next room.

She hesitated but a second, then went to the connecting door and knocked. She heard the pause in his footsteps before he came to the door and opened it.

"Have you learned anything new?" she demanded.

"No."

"Perhaps I should call Wyatt and ask him."

Dev shrugged.

"I won't be left out. This is my family—"

"And you just have to be in the know, is that it?" he broke in, anger in his eyes. "Here, this is some information Sam Waterman got for me. Maybe you'd better check it out and tell me what the clues are."

Startled, she took the envelope and opened it. After looking it over, she frowned at him. "You had Sam investigate everyone here, the family, employees, everyone."

"That's right."

"Why?"

"It should be obvious. To see who needs money."

She sat and read through the list more slowly. The information was complete, right down to their individual bank accounts. She smiled faintly. "Uncle

Clint has gambling debts. I didn't know that, but it's no surprise. He's always been kind of wild. Sophia always needs money. Cruz, Rosita, and Ruben are doing well." She handed the list back. "This is an invasion of privacy."

Dev raised an eyebrow as if mocking her sudden reticence. She didn't want to know the intimate details of other people's lives, she realized, which was probably odd for someone studying to be a psychologist.

"Afraid of knowing the truth about your friends and family?" he asked, as if reading her mind.

"Yes."

He seemed taken aback at her honesty. After placing the envelope on the writing desk in his room, he stripped out of his jacket and tie, then kicked off his shoes. Sitting in an easy chair, he studied her for a long while.

"You're sad," he finally said.

"It never goes away. Sometimes I think I'm becoming afraid of life."

"Poor little rich girl. Your father's money can't always smooth the path, can it?"

"Don't," she whispered, her throat too tight to speak. "Maybe I deserve it, but don't be sarcastic. Please."

She pressed her forehead to the door and sought control. After a long moment she spoke. "A couple of friends called this afternoon. They had lunch in San Antonio yesterday. Sophia was there, too. With a man. The description sounded like you."

"Are you asking if I was there with her?"

She hesitated, then nodded.

"I was."

The admission speared through her like a burning brand. "You shouldn't—" She stopped abruptly as she heard the accusing words fall from her lips.

His hand on her shoulder spun her around to face him. His gaze was furious, but his tone was mild. "Are you warning me to stay away from her?"

"I…" She wasn't sure what she was trying to say. "She uses people. She's dangerous and vindictive. She would use you to hurt us if she could."

"Is this jealousy talking?" he demanded, his voice deceptively soft.

She searched in her heart and was troubled by what she found. "She came between my father and the rest of the family. She hated it when he brought us presents or paid attention to any of us kids."

"I'm not your family," he reminded her. "That one incident between us…it wasn't a promise of anything more. There are no ties between us."

She felt the sweetness of their time together shatter like a Christmas angel of spun glass. She lifted her chin as the tears burned and burned behind her eyes. "I know."

Dev turned away, ashamed of his cruelty. Anger and need ate at him. He knew better than to expect anything from life, yet she made him want to grab whatever he could, to take the moments she offered and to hell with anything else. But life had a way of catching up with a person, and with it, the grief that came of believing in promises.

"Do you?" he challenged, not letting himself back down and take her into his arms to try to erase the unhappiness in her eyes. He hadn't been able to do it for his mother or his partner's wife.

"It was only an interlude." He wondered who he was trying to convince, her…or his own heart.

"You've made that clear," Vanessa said softly.

"But you don't believe me."

The silence palpitated between them as he waited for her answer. "No," she finally admitted.

Need and desolation ate him. "This conversation is pointless."

"It isn't," she quickly denied. "I just realized— you're a coward, Special Agent Devin Kincaid. You're afraid to share yourself with anyone. You're afraid of the feelings between us. The question is— why?"

He told her the blunt truth. "Because it will get messy at the end, when one of us wants to be free and the other won't let go. Because I've never seen a happy-ever-after in this life. Because there isn't such a thing."

"I see. I really do."

He touched her temple with one finger. "You see through that rose-colored cloud the poets talk about. You've led a sheltered existence—"

"Does it always have to come back to my family's money?" Vanessa demanded, impatient with his reasoning.

A ten-foot-high chain-link fence went up around him. He dropped his hand and the moment of tenderness disappeared.

"It isn't the money. It's your whole way of life. Your family is hardworking and decent, but you don't really know the world. You're young and pampered and…a delight… I'd like to take everything you think you want to give, but I'm trying to be decent about this, too.''

The moment stretched into an impasse. ''That isn't the problem.'' With that, she turned and walked out, quietly closing the door behind her as she left her room.

She headed for the stables before she did something stupid. Such as cradle him in her arms and soothe the hurts that drove him inward, angry with himself that he had slipped and let need take over his heart for one wild moment. She leaned against the railing, hating that he had been hurt, hating the cool logic he used against them…

The black sniffed at her hair, then backed off and tossed his head.

''Okay,'' she said, matching his restless mood.

She went to the tack room and brought out a saddle. The horse pranced sideways, then stilled as she talked softly. She tossed the blanket and saddle on, then cinched up quickly. In another second she was astride the stallion, and they were off into the gathering twilight, gaining speed until they flew with the wind, a tornado of need driving her on into the dark.

Dev paused near the fence. The figure leaning against the post wasn't Vanessa.

''She's gone for a ride.'' Cruz spoke up, the night shadows carving harsh angles into his face, highlighting the curve of high cheekbone.

''On the gelding?''

''She took the black.''

"You let her out on a wild stallion at night?" The fury was controllable, but barely.

The white teeth flashed in the shadowed face. The tone, when he spoke, was sardonic. "You ever try to tell a Fortune not to do something?"

"You could have stopped her. She would have listened to you." He said this as a hope, not a surety.

"Like she listened to you?" The horse trainer nodded toward the woods and the cave where the limestone bluff rose above the creek. "You know where she is. Should I saddle a mount for you?"

Dev wanted to wade into the handsome, mocking face of the ranch hand with both fists. He wanted to hit out at something, anything...

No. He wanted to hold a certain sweet vixen in his arms and gaze into eyes that promised bliss and forever and all the good things he'd missed. He hit the rail with the heel of his fist.

Walk away, his conscience warned.

Can't, another part answered.

He gazed at the woods. They seemed as dark and lonely as he felt inside. But he knew where light existed, where warmth waited for him to stroll up and catch it in his arms.

Vanessa. The stubborn part of him supplied the name.

He walked into the stable and saddled up. Perez handed him a saddlebag when he came out. "She'll need food," the man said, his face disclosing nothing.

Dev nodded. The gelding was eager to be off, and headed for the woods without direction. Dev settled into the easy rhythm of the horse and let the roan follow the trail the stallion had taken.

At the clearing, the black shook his bridle and resumed cropping grass around a boulder. The gelding chose another spot and did the same when Dev dropped the reins to the ground as Vanessa had taught him to do.

He walked up the path along the ledge.

She sat at the edge, her feet dangling over the three-story drop of the ravine. He did the same.

"Your grieving place," he said.

"Sometimes, yes."

Her smile was quick, beautiful and sad. He found he couldn't stand that. He clenched his hands on the sharp pointy jags of the ledge and held on.

"You shouldn't have followed," she told him.

"I know. I was worried about you."

"Ever the gallant protector," she said softly, wry laughter overlaying the despair.

He heard both. "I never meant it to come to this."

"You never meant to hurt me. I know."

Her words absolved him of guilt, but made him feel worse. "You don't understand, Beauty."

The word came out an endearment, recalling her reference to the Beast in the fairy tale. He hadn't meant that, either. He heaved a sigh. This wasn't going to be easy.

"Try me, FBI man."

That almost brought a smile. She was so sure they could work things out, but she didn't know and he couldn't explain. He only knew it was impossible, had always been, would always be. From the moment they'd met, from that first meeting of the eyes and the lovely verdant promise in those magic depths, he'd known he was going to fall for her and that it would be a lifetime and it wouldn't work.

But she didn't know that.

That Fortune confidence, it was part of what he loved. What she loved, what she saw, wasn't him, but a sweet and foolish notion born of romantic fantasy. If he was that fantasy for her, then he would have to live the part. For as long as it lasted.

"When you look at life too closely," he wisely explained, "it pokes you in the eye with a sharp stick."

"I know about disappointment. I understand how it feels to keep getting your expectations knocked down—"

"How?" He mocked her, but gently, knowing she hadn't a clue to the reality of his life.

One rainy night he'd stared at his father's lifeless form at the morgue and known the old man would never make one of his false promises again, that they would never be the family he and his mother had hung their hopes on.

He had watched the light dim and fade and finally flicker out in his mother who was ever the optimist, who had believed that this time they would make it as a family.

And for a while, sometimes months, once a whole year, they would be that way, long enough for him to let his guard down and begin trusting again.

That night that hope had died. Forever.

He lifted the slender hand that was capable of so much. He didn't want the light to die in her, too. Or even dim. If she thought she needed him for her happiness for a while, he would bear it. Then when she didn't, he would leave.

"No regrets," he murmured, and planted a kiss in her palm and closed her fingers around it.

"Never."

She pressed his hand to her cheek and slid it back and forth. The smooth warmth of her skin sent vibrations through him that hummed and echoed through his blood and made him remember how hope had once felt.

"Are we going to spend the night?" he asked.

"It's too dark to return."

"Let's make our bed."

They brought the blankets and saddles up to the cave and made a bed and pillows out of them. He retrieved the coffee and sandwiches from a saddlebag. They ate dinner in the light of a lone candle stuck on a small can.

"Romantic," he said, catching her gaze on him, her eyes glowing like crystals in the flickering light.

"Works for me."

Her grin was teasing, perhaps somewhat mocking of his efforts at levity. He smiled, then finished his meal and polished off the coffee. "We didn't save some for breakfast."

"I have crackers and orange juice with me. The juice is at the seep. The water will keep it cool."

"Good thinking."

"Well, a compliment from Sergeant Friday."

He reached for her. "You'll regret those words before morning," he told her.

She settled into his lap as if made for him. "Are

you going to torture me with kisses, do unspeakable
things to my body and all that?''

''You bet.''

''Good.''

They shared the toothbrush she'd stockpiled long
ago, then the orange juice and peanut butter crackers.
Vanessa yawned and stretched before mounting for
the trip back to the ranch. The peace of the night after
the wild lovemaking lingered inside her like the slum-
bering embers of an earlier crackling fire.

A hand touched her shoulder, then a finger caressed
her mouth. ''Douse the glow,'' he said. ''You'll set
the woods on fire.''

''I'm too happy.''

His smile was quick, but she saw through it. There
was something distant in him. She saw it in the bleak-
ness in his eyes, as if he saw far into their future…and
there wasn't one.

He doubted now, but he wouldn't. Someday he
would realize it was okay to dream again and to believe in them and their feelings. He was a challenge,
this doubting man. Her dark knight with the heart of
gold.

At the paddock, they brushed down the horses and
gave them each a bucket of oats before turning them
out to pasture. Across the meadow, she saw Cruz
working with one of the young cow ponies, teaching
it how to cut and spin and move the cows where he
wanted them to go.

He saw them, too, and after a second, lifted his
hand to return her wave. A blush flowed into her face.
Cruz knew they had spent the night at the cave.

"Your friend knows," Dev said, stopping behind her and slipping his hands around her waist.

"Yes."

"Does it bother you?"

She twisted around. "Why should it? We're consenting adults. Our personal life is no one's business."

"Spoken like a modern woman, one with old-fashioned values. Shall we go face the music?"

She laughed at the grim determination on his face. "We'll go take a shower, then have a real breakfast."

"Yeah, our last meal before your father shoots us."

She laughed again at his dark humor. Slipping her hand into his, she matched her stride to his longer one while he shortened his for her. Together they walked to the hacienda, slipped around to the side door and into their rooms without spotting anyone.

"Join me," she invited, and led the way to her bathroom. She tossed her clothes into the hamper and stepped into the shower. After a minute, Dev joined her.

"You have a most interesting birthmark," he said, touching her hip.

"It's how we recognize a true Fortune heir. Most of us have it."

She turned to him eagerly, ready for a new experience in this wonderful thing between a man and woman.

He examined the birthmark then took her face between his hands while the water splashed merrily over them. "Shall we?" he murmured, and hovered an inch above her lips as he waited for her reply.

"I would be very disappointed if we didn't."

"That's why I came prepared."

He placed the foil packet in the soap dish and, taking up the bar, lathered them both all over. She formed a new concept about the idea of cleanliness.

Two hours later, Ryan met in the study with the agent as usual. "What are you checking now?" he asked.

"Bank accounts, personal financial history."

The agent was nothing if not succinct. Ryan hid his impatience in the face of the other man's seemingly endless attention to detail. "And?"

"There are some interesting facts that have turned up."

"What are they?"

"I'd rather not discuss it now, sir. If you don't mind."

The fact that this was said with unfailing courtesy, as always, also grated on his nerves. The agent stayed busy all the time, looking, checking, double-checking. Nothing was coming of it that he could see. He reined in the feelings of impotence and helplessness. If the FBI hadn't given up, neither would he.

"Fine." He poured himself a cup of coffee and refreshed Dev's mug from the coffeemaker in his office. "Perhaps we can talk about you and my daughter."

The agent didn't move a muscle. Neither did he speak.

Ryan thought he should have listened to Lily and not gone down this road. But he was concerned about Vanessa and he wasn't about to back down in front of the younger man.

"I, um, saw you returning to the house this morning...before the sun came up. Vanessa wasn't at dinner last night. I didn't know you had returned to the ranch."

The agent nodded.

"I don't want her hurt."

"Neither do I."

The man returned his stare without so much as a muscle twitch. "You ever play poker?" Ryan asked.

For the first time a smile, somewhat rueful, broke over the stoic features. "No, sir, I never had the time or inclination to gamble with my money."

"Only with your life?"

"I take calculated risks, not foolish ones."

"Hmm." Ryan sipped the hot, strong coffee and mulled over how to gracefully exit this discussion. "Do you love her?" he asked suddenly.

That brought a flash of emotion into the younger man's eyes that startled him. For a second he looked into stark desolation, then it was gone.

He had depth and secrets Ryan figured the agent didn't share with anyone, not even with his lover, who happened to be *his* daughter. What a mess he was making of this interview, he acknowledged glumly. Lily had tried to warn him.

"There are...feelings," the agent admitted.

A very cool customer. Ryan liked the man in spite of his worries about his daughter. He felt she was vulnerable right now due to the kidnapping. "Vanessa is very strong on family and all that entails, ties and loyalty, all that."

Dev nodded. "I'm aware of that, sir." He couldn't for the life of him figure out where this conversation was going, and he sure as hell wasn't going to volunteer anything to Vanessa's father.

The man was worried. Join the club. Dev was pretty worried himself. He couldn't allow her to interfere with the investigation, but he couldn't ignore her. Sometime during the night, he had decided he could juggle the two elements of his life, but he wouldn't mingle them. The hours they shared would have to be taken from their real lives, but that would be okay. He could handle it.

"There is one thing," her father said.

Ryan watched him with that hawkish gaze that could easily wring a confession from guilty souls such as his young sons...and a man old enough to know better but who was lover to his daughter.

"I ask that, if the time ever comes, you let her down easy. Will you do that?"

Dev sorted through the confusion the words caused. If the time ever comes? It was a surety. She would get tired of playing games with him at some point. When it happened, she would be truthful with him, but gentle. And he would let her go as gracefully as he could.

It was an easy promise to make. "Of course." He picked up a tablet. It was time for business. "Did the sheriff and his men go over every inch of ground around the main house?"

Eight

"Just what are we looking for?"

Vanessa stretched her weary back. Bending over for hours, staring at the ground, was not her idea of an investigation, especially after spending the night lying on the ground. Although being in Dev's arms had been heavenly.

"Clues."

"This has all been done before," she reminded him. "Wyatt and his men were very thorough."

Dev straightened and looked at her, but said nothing.

She sighed. "Yeah, the spoiled brat syndrome."

He chuckled. "The Fortune impatience."

"That sounds better."

She sat on one of the boulders beside the dry creek in the front courtyard and shook a pebble from her shoe. Dev patiently turned over every rock and fallen leaf. His white shirt strained across his shoulders as he bent to his task again. His jeans outlined the hard thighs and buttocks.

Her adult life had been more attuned to books and thinking than the physical, but now she found herself acutely aware of his body and her own. She wanted to be near him all the time. He never left her thoughts.

Dreamily, she watched as he slowly filtered

through every phase of their lives and the daily routine of the ranch. He knew every chore to be done and who performed it. He knew who went where and when they came back. He knew things he wasn't telling her.

Some of it was about them.

She had tried to tactfully draw him out about his morning chats with her father, but he only smiled and shook his head at her inquisition.

But his eyes...they made her want to weep. Instead of their intimacy dispelling the loneliness, it had only increased, drawing him deeper into himself even while he smiled and teased her.

Oh, if only you could see what I see, she wanted to cry. What a fine, decent person you are, the life we could share, the future we could build...

But she couldn't tell him. He would have to find the truth for himself if they were to ever have a chance.

"So take what the day presents and make the most of it," she said aloud.

He glanced her way again, his eyes dark and quiet and so very gentle in his regard of her. He broke her heart.

Sobered by her thoughts, she started searching once more. They worked until noon, then stopped in the glaring heat of the day and retreated inside. Dev worked alone in the office after a quick lunch. When she took him a fresh glass of iced tea at three, she overheard him talking to his boss.

"No, nothing," he said. He murmured a thanks to her, then went back to his phone conversation.

She lingered, wanting to be near him. The futile

search had deepened her anguish about Baby Bryan. She couldn't—wouldn't believe he was dead. But she worried about him.

"The end of the month," Dev said. He flicked her a glance before running a finger down the desk calendar.

Her heart gave a giant lurch. She pressed a hand to her chest. Dev frowned slightly. She turned to leave, knowing he didn't like her invading the office.

"Wait," he said.

She glanced over her shoulder. He motioned her to come back. She crossed the room, her feet heavy. She could sense bad news a mile away.

He looped one arm around her waist while he finished his conversation. When he hung up, he pulled her into his lap. Surprised, she leaned against the chair arm and watched his eyes roam her face.

"It won't be the end of the world," he said quietly, "when I leave."

"When?"

"You heard." His eyes scolded her for refusing to see the truth.

"The end of the month." She repeated his words. "Then you'll be assigned elsewhere?"

He hesitated. "I'm already working on other things."

She couldn't hide her surprise. "What?"

"An old case that recently reopened. I'm sifting through reports, looking for the odd tidbit that might tell us something to go with the new information."

"Was it a kidnapping?"

He shook his head. "Gun running."

"That sounds dangerous."

He smiled and rubbed a strand of hair between his thumb and finger. "All life is like that."

"Yours was. It doesn't have to be that way." She wanted desperately to convince him. "There can be peace and contentment. There can be shared goals and mutual trust as well as respect."

His eyes were kind, but disbelieving. "For some."

"But not for you." She didn't know how to break through thirty-seven years of doubt.

"Not for my partner, my best friend," he said. "He died, taking a shot for me. He left a wife and two kids behind. When I first joined the FBI, the agent I replaced had lost his wife and kid when the bad guys came after him at his home."

She made soothing sounds and wished she could bring rest to his tortured spirit. "That isn't common. Very few families of law enforcement officials have ever been subjected to violence because of their spouses' jobs."

"But some are. I vowed never to allow that to happen to anyone I knew—"

"By never letting anyone get that close," she ended, the sadness dipping deep within her. "No one could hurt the person you love because you decided not to love anyone. Except," she added, "you made an error, Mr. FBI man, you fell in love with me."

A shadow dropped over his face. "We became lovers."

She laid her fingers over his lips, then lingered to trace the outline, recalling how much pleasure he could give with his mouth…

"Stop it," he ordered, giving her a shake.

"Stop remembering how much we've shared?

Never, Dev. There is nothing you can do to diminish our time together. Please don't be sorry." She cupped his beloved face between her hands. "Promise me you won't be sorry."

She held his gaze, saw the struggle in his eyes, felt the lowering sensation inside when he at last smiled in that heart-twisting way he had.

"I'll never have regrets. I told you that."

"But do you believe it?"

He kissed her for an answer.

At five, Dev yawned and pushed his hat off his forehead. Vanessa ignored the sweat meandering between her breasts. The air was dead still. The temperature was in the hundreds...again—the tenth straight day of high heat. Ranchers were worried about their cattle, farmers about their crops.

"I give up," he said aloud.

Vanessa rolled her eyes. "The FBI never gives up. It's in the code."

"Well, I'm retiring for the day, then."

"Huh."

She continued her hunt along the ground between the house and paloverde. Dev had said it was probably too far away from the windows, but she reasoned that the kidnapper might have stood in the light shade, such as it was from the thin bladed leaves of the desert tree, until his accomplice had signaled him to get the baby.

Noticing one of the tiny spotlights was slanted toward the ground instead of up into the tree, she stopped her search, plopped on a rock and leaned over to see if she could bend it into the correct position.

Yes, it moved easily. Satisfied at doing something useful, she huffed out a breath that seemed as hot as all of Texas was these days. Crossing her arms on her knees, she rested her chin on them. Staring into the gravel around the spotlight, she noticed a coppery gleam among the stones.

She picked it up and studied it. "Dev, come here. I've found something."

"What?"

"A rowel from a spur. It has a medallion from a rodeo mounted on one side. The medallion is dated last year. 'Calf roping champion,' it says. Hmm."

"Don't pick it up," he said.

"Too late."

He strode over, whipped a plastic bag from his pocket and told her to drop it in.

She did with a grimace. "I probably messed up any fingerprints, didn't I?"

"Maybe. Maybe not."

His noncommittal answer fueled her disgust with herself. She knew better than to touch evidence with her bare hands. The worry about Baby Bryan, never far from her mind, rose to haunt her. "I'm sorry," she said.

He hooked a finger under her chin. "Don't beat yourself up about it. Let's go to town and see what we can find out about this." He held up the bag.

"Perhaps I should stay here. I'll only be in the way."

"Don't go humble on me, Beauty. I'll think you've been taken over by aliens."

After giving him a scolding punch on the shoulder, she went with him to his car. A little more than an hour later, they were ensconced on high stools at the crime lab in San Antonio.

Charlie Fong, the crime lab specialist, held the rowel in a clamp and studied the medallion. "I'll run prints first. You want me to check for blood, too?"

"If you don't mind."

Charlie grinned. "Well, I do, since it's past time for me to go home and I'm hungry, but I already called my wife and warned her I'll be late. She said I had better eat before coming home. She won't save my supper."

Dev's smile was wry. "Okay, okay, I get the hint. Chinese?"

"Yeah. Don't forget the hot mustard."

Dev took her elbow. "Come on. I've got to feed him. We may as well eat, too."

They went to a Chinese take-out place near the Alamo. Tourists roamed the streets, forming a steady stream up and down the stairs to the riverwalk. The last rays of sunlight, reflecting off the tall buildings that surrounded the adobe Alamo, shimmered in the stagnant heat.

"Being in town feels like being in an oven," Vanessa remarked. She placed the white bag on the floor between her feet. "The ranch never seems this hot, even if the air temperature is the same."

"The concrete holds the heat."

He looked distracted, his thoughts turned inward. She wondered what he thought the rowel might disclose. She was afraid to hope that it might lead them directly to one of the kidnappers, yet she couldn't bear the thought that it wouldn't help at all.

"Do you think—"

"It's better not to," he said before she finished. He glanced at her after stopping at a traffic light. "If you don't pin your hopes on any one thing, then you're not disappointed if it fails."

He sounded wise, but it was wisdom born from pain. Dev had learned never to let himself hope for anything.

They returned to the crime lab in silence. Charlie turned a triumphant smile on them.

"Got a print," he said.

"How clear?"

"Perfect."

"Check it against Vanessa's," Dev requested.

"I forgot and picked it up when I found it," she confessed when the lab specialist glanced her way.

She liked watching Dev with other men. There was an easy camaraderie between him and the technician. He and Wyatt got along, too. Her father never missed a morning conference and, if Dev was absent for dinner, asked about him. She liked knowing other men respected him.

"Dinner?"

She blinked out of her introspection and accepted a plate. The three of them sat on the stools around an empty lab table and ate the meal. "Mmm, I love sweet and sour pork. And noodles."

"Ah, yes," Charlie agreed, nodding his head. "That plate you're using recently held the brain of a criminal. We were trying to find out what poison killed him."

"My plate?" she croaked in pretend horror.

Charlie considered. "Well, maybe it was the one Kincaid is using."

Dev lofted one eyebrow at their joking and stuck a piece of pork into his mouth with the chopsticks. He was adept at using them and not at all perturbed by any previous use of the borrowed lab plate.

"When do we take my fingerprints?" she asked.

"I have them on file," Charlie told her.

She couldn't hide her surprise.

"I have everyone at the main ranch house," Dev told her. His eyes locked with hers.

"Everyone is suspect," she said, the sadness welling up in her. "It hurts to doubt people I've known and loved all my life. I can't believe it could be anyone at the ranch."

"People are funny," Charlie advised her, his eyes going solemn. "Especially about money."

"I never realized it was such a problem until now. Until the kidnapping," she added, lifting a piece of pork.

Dev pushed her hand toward her mouth. "Eat," he advised. "Don't think so much."

Charlie finished first and went back to work. "Good news," he called. "You only left a smudge along the edge. More good news. The print belongs to the one found at the motel."

Charlie slid back from the computer to give Dev a clear view of the screen. Dev shoved his stool back and strode across the lab in four brisk strides. Satisfaction and excitement beat through him.

"What?" Vanessa demanded, crowding in beside him, touching him all the way along their sides. "The fingerprint you found on the motel table matches the one on the rowel?"

"Perfectly," Charlie assured her.

Dev kept an eye on her as she stared at the screen, her mouth open slightly as she took in the implications. "This ties the person at the hotel to someone on the ranch."

"The person at the motel was the kidnapper," Dev murmured close to her ear.

"Yes, but there was someone else, too."

It hurt to look into her eyes, to see the slow death of trust as she put two and two together and correctly came up with… "An inside job, just as you noted on your list," he reminded her gently.

"But this makes it real. Someone had to help the person grab the baby, someone who knew where everyone was, then gave a signal to this person." She waved a hand toward the rowel and its unknown owner.

"I think the baby was handed out the window, probably put into a duffel bag or something that someone could carry without being noticed, then taken to a nearby vehicle."

"Someone who was there to pack his bags and head off for the rodeo circuit," Vanessa concluded. "Only he went into hiding. With the baby. But who helped him?"

When she gazed up at him, all the hurt of betrayal in her eyes, Dev was lost. He put his arm around her shoulders and held her, feeling the misery reflected in her eyes.

"We'll find him," he said huskily.

Charlie looked from one to the other and cleared his throat. "Dev's the best," he said. "He'll figure it out and nab the guy."

She nodded and smiled faintly. "Of course. The FBI always gets their man."

Dev could have kissed her. She was brave and caring and all the things that made him yearn for all the good things in life, to believe they were possible...

"What next?" she asked.

"Next we go find every person who was in the motel out on the interstate on April sixth."

"Wyatt checked everyone out—"

"But maybe something was overlooked, just as the rowel was missed in the previous search. Maybe we can find out what name our cowboy used at that time."

"And a car tag," Charlie put in.

"But the police have already checked out everyone they could find."

"We'll check them again," Dev promised. "And maybe we'll find out something about the person who rented the room for those three nights."

Doubts darkened her eyes. She sighed as if weary beyond hope. "Okay, let's go do it."

Dev spared a rueful glance at the rest of his meal and placed his hand on the small of her back. "We'll start in the morning."

Vanessa sighed and slumped in the easy chair in Dev's room. He settled in the desk chair. She couldn't summon a smile, not even for him. "I feel as if I'm at the bottom of the pit."

"I know."

"Because you've been there." She reached over and brushed the dark wing of hair off his forehead.

"It must be hard to never let yourself expect good things, to never let yourself dream or hope."

"Don't go psychological."

"I'm stating an observation, not probing."

"Okay."

He wouldn't argue with her. It almost made her angry with him. She shifted restlessly. "I need something. I'm filled with yearning, and I don't even know why."

No answer.

"Closure," she finally decided. "I'm a person who needs closure. I want to solve the case, get my nephew back and get on with life."

Dev flicked her a glance. His expression disclosed nothing, not even the sadness that lived within him and weighed so heavily on her heart.

"Tell me to shut up and quit complaining," she urged, clutching at the ragged edges of humor.

"You have a right," he said quietly.

Tears burned behind her eyes. At times he was the kindest person she had ever known. Because he knew what it was to hurt.

"I love you," she whispered, the words catching in her throat. "It's the only good to come out of this—that we met and fell in love."

"It would be nice to think so."

"But you know differently."

"I know that bad things, like good things, don't last forever. If you remember that, you'll make it through the pit and back to the light."

She gazed into the courtyard. She had lived here all her life, except for the time spent at college.

"Home," she murmured. "It beckons with the

force of all the memories I've collected here. It was my safe place, but then my mother got sick and we were invaded by evil—''

"Enter the wicked stepmother," he put in. No smile eased the sober lines of his face.

"I had never disliked anyone before. It was a strange feeling, not to trust someone in my home. And now this—another person on the ranch with evil in his heart, someone who would take a baby—''

Her voice broke and she couldn't go on. She closed her eyes. After a moment she felt his arms slide around her.

"We'll find the snake," he promised softly, putting her across his lap. "And drive him out of Eden."

She leaned her head against the winged back and stared into his eyes, which seemed navy blue in the deep twilight. "And then you'll leave?"

"I'll have to."

The deep, sad certainty in him fed the desolation inside her. "Why can't this one thing last? Why can't we have this? Make me understand."

"Ah, Beauty," he said, then hesitated.

The sadness was in his eyes again. For her, she realized. He didn't want to hurt her, but he wouldn't give her false hope, either.

"Do you realize you made a promise a moment ago?" She stroked her hands along his shoulders. Such broad shoulders. They could carry the weight of the world. He was a rescuer, and he could no more ignore his nature than she could stop being an optimist, even if she was in the dumps now.

"It's my job," he explained gently. "I cast out

snakes. Or at least try to put them behind bars for a good portion of their lives.''

"A paladin," she murmured, "who travels the world and stamps out evil.''

"Nothing so noble as that," Dev denied.

She thumped him on the chest. "Yes, it is. Don't be denigrating the person I love, hear?''

He kissed her hand, then held it against his chest. "You almost make me believe in fairy tales," he whispered, his face hidden in her hair.

He inhaled deeply and stroked through the strands, smoothing the tangles caused by their day's work, fluttering the wispy curls at her temples, making her shiver.

"Believe, Dev. I need you to believe. My well of faith is running low." Her smile trembled on her lips, then she gave it up.

"I know, Beauty. I know.''

Nine

Dev laid the pen aside and squeezed the bridge of his nose, trying to dispel the headache that insisted on pounding behind his eyes. The door to the study opened and closed quietly. Ryan Fortune sat in a leather chair and looked at him.

"Good morning," he said. "I've been talking to my daughter." He raised his eyebrows in question.

Dev wondered if they were going to continue the discussion of his involvement with Vanessa.

"I understand you have good news about the kidnapping."

Dev relaxed slightly. "Some news, at any rate. I don't know whether it's good or not. Did Vanessa tell you about the rowel she found?"

Ryan shook his head. "She said I should check with you. She didn't know if you wanted the information known."

Recalling the episode with Hubcap Johnson and his confession, Dev had to smile. She was learning. He described the rowel. "I'm waiting for Wyatt to let me know who the winner of the calf roping was at that particular rodeo. It may tie in with the name registered at the motel or with the cowboy who worked here. It may give us a real name if the others were aliases."

Ryan helped himself to coffee. "There's a Native American in Leather Bucket who handcrafts boots. He also makes spurs and customizes them for cowboys."

"Customizes?"

"Yeah. Cowboys like to wear their medals from the rodeo circuit as good-luck pieces. Some have them mounted on the rowels of their spurs. Tomahawk will do it for them."

Dev picked up the pen and pulled a notepad toward him. "Know how I can locate this guy?"

"The Leather Bucket Saddle Shop takes orders for him. He stops in and picks them up once in a while. You can call them for his whereabouts."

Dev picked up the phone and called information for the number of the shop. Ryan smiled wryly and headed for the door. "I can see you're eager to get on the job."

After writing down the address of the saddle shop, Dev put away his notes and locked the desk. He walked around the ornate recliner and looked into the courtyard. The maid was making her rounds of the rooms, cleaning and straightening up after the Fortune clan. He had to admit, a person could get used to being pampered real fast.

His blood speeded up when he saw Vanessa standing by the fountain. She was talking to her uncle Clint.

Dev frowned. He didn't like the man. Not that he had anything against him. But...he didn't like him. He didn't mention this to Vanessa. She would simply jump to the man's defense as she did for everyone on the ranch. She couldn't believe anyone on the premises would want to hurt another person. They were all one big happy family.

Except for the person who had a grudge against them.

"You and the FBI agent seem to be keeping close company these days."

Vanessa glanced at her uncle and smiled. "I'm helping with the case by writing a profile of the kidnappers. He doesn't seem to appreciate my advice."

"A difficult person, huh? I've never known anyone who could hold out against the Fortune charm for long."

An uneasy feeling ran down her spine. She couldn't tell if Uncle Clint was being sarcastic or not. There had been just a bit of an edge to his words. However, his smile was without guile. She was becoming as suspicious of everyone as Dev was.

"Dev's got a cast-iron heart."

As soon as the words were out, she regretted them.

"Ah, you can't bend him to your will?" he teased.

She wrinkled her nose in mock dismay. "He thinks I'm the spoiled daughter of the house and should return to my tea parties or whatever and get out of his hair. He should know that Fortunes don't give up that easily."

"Yeah," Clint said. "He should."

Vanessa observed the thinning of her uncle's lips and the hard set of his jaw. He slapped a willow switch against the stone edge of the fountain.

Agitation, she diagnosed, rather than absentminded fidgeting. Her uncle was tense.

"Is there any word at all?" he suddenly demanded.

"God, I'm sick of this waiting for a call or something from the kidnappers. What the hell are they doing?" *Slap, slap.*

She touched his shoulder in sympathy. "I wish I knew."

"I can't see that the damned FBI is doing a thing."

"They are. Dev is. He's…checking every fact over again."

Slap. "Wyatt had every deputy in the county do that. Not to mention Ryan had Sam Waterman guarding the ranch and Lily's place as if they were the national mint." *Slap.*

She sighed in despair. "I know. It's so frustrating."

"Hasn't the agent come up with anything new?" *Slap. Slap. Slap.*

For a second she was tempted to tell him about the rowel. After all, he was a relative. Baby Bryan was his great-nephew.

"Why would the FBI stay on the case if they didn't know something?" *Slap.*

The sound grated on her nerves, but she didn't tell him to stop. Tamping back the impulse to explain everything to him, she shook her head. "I don't know."

He gave her a sharp glance. His eyes were blue and surrounded by long curling lashes that were gorgeous. However, his body was honed into toughness by his years of ranch work, giving a lie to the pretty-boy appearance of his face. He had a way of jutting his chin out and holding his mouth that was sort of arrogant. He looked that way now.

"Well, look who's here," he muttered.

She turned to see. Her heart pounded like mad as

Dev approached them. His eyes flicked over her, leaving prickles along every nerve in her body. The scent of his aftershave lightly wafted around her as he stopped beside them. He was like the cool breath of a morning breeze.

"Good morning," he greeted them in his gravely polite way, his face pleasant but unrevealing.

She was glad she hadn't told her father and uncle about the new clue. Dev wouldn't have liked it.

"You heard anything?" Clint demanded.

"Nothing from the kidnappers."

Dev made a quick survey of the other man. Lockhart was dressed in work clothes and smelled of horses and leather, which was not an unpleasant odor, he had discovered.

Especially when it was combined with Vanessa's sweet scent. He was very familiar with the colognes she wore—not perfume because animals were sensitive to strong smells, she had explained. The sun was heating up the courtyard, making it easy for him to detect the roses and jasmine among the attractive plantings.

He glanced at Vanessa, a question in his eyes. "I need to go to town."

"I'd like to come, too," she quickly said. "If that's okay."

He nodded, aware that her uncle took in every word. He sighed internally. Probably every person on the ranch knew they were lovers by now. Apparently they hadn't done a very good job of concealing their involvement. He wondered if he would get another lecture about letting her down easy.

"How long are you going to hang around here?" Lockhart demanded, his chin thrust out.

Dev resisted an urge to punch the man. "As long as it takes," he replied, careful to keep any inflection of anger from his tone.

Lockhart gave an impatient snort.

Maybe it was the land, not family genetics, that made the hill country Texans impatient.

"I'll get my purse."

He subdued a smile as Vanessa hurried off, ready to pursue whatever path opened before her.

"What's with you and my niece?"

Ah, the expected inquisition. Apparently every man on the place was protective of the young heiress. He gave Lockhart a frigid look and said nothing.

The man's eyes narrowed. He flicked his hair, which was brown with red highlights, off his face as the breeze picked up. Vanessa's fiery tresses came from her Lockhart genes.

Dev checked the sky. Clouds were forming. There would be an afternoon thunderstorm. He wanted to get to town and talk with the sheriff and the old man who made good-luck pieces into spurs for cowboys.

"Just watch that you don't overstep yourself," Lockhart warned with a snarl, and strode off. He exited the courtyard through the garage door.

Dev mulled the threat over on the way to his SUV. The man had a chip on his shoulder about something. A grudge against the family?

According to local gossip, Clint had been furious when his father had sold their hundred-thousand-acre ranch to the Double Crown. He'd been a kid at the time, but he had made it plain he expected to inherit the place and run it. His father had been a competent attorney, but a lousy rancher.

A carouser and hothead, Clint Lockhart had been a handful as a boy. As a man, he lived in a cabin about a mile from the Perez house and still had an interesting social life. Dev wondered if the Fortune patriarch knew his brother-in-law was one of his wife's lovers. One among many, Dev added.

The lovely Sophia got around, one might say.

"Okay, I'm ready. Sorry, I had a call from my sister."

He nodded, only half listening to her chatter. He simply liked the sound of her voice with its unfailing good humor, her concern for others a deeper chord running through the melody of her words.

Swallowing against the knot that rose in his throat, he admitted he was getting sucked in. She was the one thing he couldn't refuse. Knowing it was hopeless didn't stop the need, didn't dim the glow that came from her light shining into his heart. Ah, God…

"There's Dallas," Vanessa said. "Blow the horn." She reached over his arm and gave a couple of taps.

Dallas, repairing a section of fence along the drive that led to his house, looked up and waved. The young widower was only two years older than Vanessa. His wife had died a couple of years ago in childbirth. As far as Dev could tell, the young man never dated, rarely left the ranch, and lived the life of a recluse in his adobe home, which was a smaller rendition of the main house.

"He's lonely," Vanessa murmured, looking back at her brother with a worried expression. She settled in the seat with a sigh. "Like you, he's shut himself off from close attachment to anyone else. He was devastated when Sara died. The baby was stillborn.''

Dev steeled himself against the emotions her sorrow generated. "Life can be tough," was all he said.

"Yes,"

He hated the thread of sadness that sometimes overlaid the lilt in her voice. He wanted to smooth life's path for her so she would always be happy. But that was wishful thinking. He hadn't been able to do a thing for his mother or for Stan's wife. The cost of living was pain. The truth was as simple and inescapable as that.

"What are we doing in town?" she asked.

"We're not going to San Antonio. Your father told me about a man in Leather Bucket who might be able to help us with the rowel.''

"Oh, Mr. Tomahawk, of course," she said.

"Why didn't you mention him?"

"I didn't think of him in connection with kidnapping. He's ancient. I'd be surprised if he's still in business.''

"He was in last week," the man at the saddle shop told them. "He'll drop off his new stuff in a couple of weeks.''

"You know where he lives?"

"Sure. Take the old El Paso highway out past the new church, take a left at the intersection, go about five miles, then look for a road that drops off sharply to the right into a narrow limestone canyon. Old Tom lives at the end of the road.''

"Let's pick up lunch and some drinks," Vanessa suggested. "It's a long drive.''

"Five miles?"

She laughed. "You'll see."

They stopped at a local diner in Leather Bucket and ordered club sandwiches to go. Dev bought a foam cooler and put a six-pack of soda and a bag of ice inside.

The highway was paved, but old and potholed. Dev found the top safe speed was around forty. They passed the church. A half mile later he turned left at an intersection. The road was gravel instead of blacktop.

It went around a curve and the road narrowed to about one and half lanes. Another quarter mile and it petered out into one lane. They wound around blind curves and limestone outcroppings. He had to stop twice to roll boulders that had fallen from a rocky bluff out of the way.

Their speed averaged ten miles an hour on the good parts. Vanessa snickered when he stopped for the third time.

Dev surveyed the winding road behind them. They had picked up a tail when they'd left Leather Bucket. He wondered who was following them and why. The road was dangerous in and of itself. He didn't want to enact a chase for their lives, too.

It took the better part of an hour, but they finally came upon a tiny adobe house set in a grove of native oaks. The narrow valley was verdant at this end. There was a fruit and pecan orchard, plus a lush garden.

An old woman in a large straw hat and a long skirt picked beans. Her smile was toothless when she straightened and waved to them. She headed for the house.

"Is Mr. Tomahawk in?" Vanessa asked politely.

"In his shop. He is working," the old woman explained. "Come with me."

She led them around the house to a log structure with a canvas roof. An old man, his face as furrowed as the country they had just driven through, rose to greet them.

"Mr. Tomahawk, I'm Vanessa Fortune. You know my father," Vanessa said. "Once, when I was young, I met you at the saddle shop in Leather Bucket."

Dev raised his eyebrows at her formal manner of speaking.

The old man nodded. "There were two of you."

"Yes, my twin, Victoria, was with us."

"Your father is well?"

"Yes, thank you. This is Special Agent Devin Kincaid with the FBI. My father's grandson has been stolen. Mr. Kincaid is helping us find him."

The old woman gave a keening cry and made the sign of the cross as if to ward off any evil they might have brought into the peaceful valley. Dev thought of the person following them and felt guilty.

"This is a sad thing. How can I help you?" The old man looked his way.

Dev removed a photo from his pocket and showed the picture of the rowel to the craftsman.

Tomahawk nodded at once. "This I have seen."

"Do you know the man who ordered the medal mounted on a spur?" he asked. "Did you see him?"

The old man turned to his wife and spoke in his native tongue. She nodded. "I will return," she said.

After she went into the house, the old man brought chairs for them. They sat in the shade of the hogan. Vanessa exclaimed over the boots set neatly in a row on a shelf.

"These men died before they could claim them," he said. "I make one pair a month now. When I was younger, I could do a pair in two, maybe three, days. I am thinking of retiring and drawing the social security my grandson has told me about. But I don't know. It is good to be busy."

Dev suppressed a startled snort. The man was ninety if he was a day. The old lady...she might be a young eighty-nine. He wondered how long they had been married.

His gaze went to Vanessa. Her fiery red tresses contrasted brilliantly with the old man's long white hair, neatly braided at his nape, as they examined a pair of boots from the shelf.

"Dev, I think these would fit you," she told him, holding up a pair of black boots with intricate carvings of tan in the leather. "Try them on."

The next thing he knew he'd bought a pair of fancy boots for a thousand bucks. "They'll last forever if you take care of them," she assured him.

"At this price, they'd better last two lifetimes," he murmured while writing out the check. He'd have to transfer funds from his savings by phone when he returned to the ranch. "Don't cash this for a day or two," he advised.

The old man gave him a gummy grin. "Bossy woman."

"You got that right."

"He loves it," Vanessa told Mr. Tomahawk.

Mrs. Tomahawk brought an order form from the house. She also brought a pot of tea sweetened with the honey from wild bees, she told them. Perspiration soaked the back of Dev's shirt while he sipped the brew. A sheen of moisture glowed from Vanessa's face. The old couple didn't sweat a drop.

Mr. Tomahawk studied the order, then handed it to Dev. On it was a picture of the medallion attached to the rowel.

"Yes, this is the one, but the man's name doesn't match the cowboy's or the hotel guest's names."

"He used a lot of aliases?" Vanessa suggested.

Dev spoke to the couple. "May I keep this? I'd like to have the handwriting to compare to another."

"Yes, but I must have it back. For the taxes. My grandson is an accountant. He says we must have paper. A handshake is no good anymore."

The many lines in his face slanted sorrowfully. Dev knew the feeling. Sometimes, dealing only with the bad facets of society, he began to believe there were no honest people left.

And then he had met Vanessa Fortune and the promise of springtime had fallen into his arms. He cast her a worried glance, before speaking to his host.

"Is there a way to go back without using the road we came in on?" He didn't have any hope that there was.

"Yes, but it is rough," the old man warned.

Dev laughed wryly. "Worse than that one?" He nodded toward the gravel road.

The wife laughed behind her hand. "If you keep on this road, you will come to a place where the spring flows. There, you will look up and see the way.''

Dev thanked them for their help and hospitality. Tucking the order form into a plastic bag and storing it safely in the inner pocket of his suit, he led the way to the SUV. They took off down the canyon.

"Oh, my heavens," Vanessa murmured when they came to the spring. They did, indeed, have to look up. A trail, apparently made by wagon tracks, angled at an impossible slant along the rock face.

Dev switched to four-wheel drive and dropped the gear into its lowest range. "If a mule pulling a wagon can make it, so can we," he reasoned.

"Why are we going this way? At least we knew how bad it was on the other road."

"I never like to take the same path twice."

He didn't tell her he was worried about an ambush waiting around one of the many bends on the narrow road back to town. If he'd been alone, he would have relished the chance to possibly catch the person who had followed them. But not with Vanessa along.

She was silent as they started up the trail. Dev carefully kept the truck tires in the twin ruts that formed the road. From the corner of his eye, he saw her knuckles whiten as she clutched the edge of the seat, but there wasn't a peep out of her.

Pride swelled his chest. She was so brave.

A half hour later they came out at the top of the canyon wall. The trail widened and, under the shade of an oak that looked as gnarled and ancient as the couple they had left, he stopped. "Let's have lunch."

"I can't," she said. "My hands won't let go."

He laughed at her admission of fear and popped

the top on a cool can of soda. She accepted it quick enough. They ate lunch there at the lip of the canyon and listened to the quiet. Only wind and the rustle of tree leaves interrupted the peace of the moment.

Across the narrow canyon, Dev picked out the trail of dust caused by another vehicle on the gravel road toward the couple's home. He watched until he was sure it was heading back toward town.

After eating, they traveled another quarter mile and picked up a gravel road that turned into a paved one, then joined the highway back into Leather Bucket. He didn't relax until he had the Fortune heiress in a traffic jam caused by a faulty stoplight.

"Ah, civilization," he murmured, then laughed, pleased that he'd at least thwarted the other guy.

"Was there someone following us?" Vanessa asked, her face pensive when she turned to him. "That was why we came back a different way, wasn't it?"

He couldn't lie to her. "Yes."

The brilliant green of her eyes clouded. "Why? Who hates us this much?"

He didn't explain that there were probably many people who hated them simply because of who they were and all that they had. "Envy is a hateful thing."

"And dangerous."

"Don't worry about it," he said soothingly. "We'll find the snake and make Eden safe once more."

She smiled at him, but her eyes were downcast. She was learning there was more than one beast in the world.

Vanessa watched Wyatt study the new evidence. He removed the card the cowboy had signed at the motel from the case folder. "Ah," he said.

"Same initials," Dev remarked, looking over his shoulder.

"Yeah. He probably has a belt buckle with J.M. on it, so he chooses names to go with that."

"The handwriting is the same," Vanessa noted from the other side of the sheriff's chair. "Look at the slant of the letters. The 'J' on James, Jerry and Jeremy has no loop, just a downstroke like a spear."

Dev nodded. "Ruben said the man took a lot of ribbing at the bunkhouse with a name like James Madison."

Wyatt pulled the card and order form closer and peered at the signatures on each. "The name he used at the ranch might be the real one. He had a social security number to go with it."

"They can be obtained with a fake birth certificate," Dev said. "He could have several."

Wyatt bounced a pencil, eraser end down, on his desk, catching it each time it rebounded. "I could get a court order to check his account for an address."

Dev nodded. "We need all the help we can get."

"What will that help?" Vanessa asked, discouragement eating at her.

"It may get us a permanent address. Someone there may be able to tell us something." Wyatt shrugged, then bounced the pencil again. "He's our only lead."

"Our only unknown, at any rate," Dev added. "I need to make a copy of the order and send it to the Tomahawks for their file."

"Are those Tomahawk boots?" Wyatt demanded, rising and staring over the desk at Dev's boots.

"Yeah. They ought to be gold-plated for the price." He gave Vanessa a stern glance for talking him into such an extravagance.

Wyatt snorted. "I'd give my left arm to have a pair. The waiting list has over a hundred people on it. Tomahawk boots will last a lifetime."

"That's what I told him," Vanessa put in. She explained how Dev got the boots.

"That road is terrible," Wyatt mused, a gleam in his eyes. "Maybe I'll mosey out that way tomorrow and return his receipt in person."

"It seems a bit morbid to buy a dead man's boots," Dev mentioned.

"Why?" Wyatt tossed the pencil into a cup that held an assortment of writing utensils. "He won't need them."

He grinned unrepentantly as Dev grimaced. Vanessa patted Dev's shoulder. "I didn't realize you were so sensitive."

She assumed an innocent expression at his glare.

"If you really are going out to Tomahawk's place," Dev said, returning to business, "you might see if you can pick up a set of tire prints. Someone followed us out there."

Wyatt's smile faded. "I'll do better than that. I'll send a deputy out that way now. There's a storm brewing, according to the weatherman. Tornado warnings are out in the northern part of the state now. It's supposed to hit here by nightfall."

"Hmm, we had better head out, then. I'd appreciate any help you can give us on our missing cowboy. He's been underground for over six weeks. That seems strange behavior for a rodeo rider."

"I'll keep in touch," the sheriff promised.

Vanessa said goodbye to her friend after the two men shook hands. "Take care," she murmured, and kissed his cheek.

"You, too." He walked with them to the big room where several deputies worked at their desks. "Tanberg, can I see you a minute?" he called. "Bring your partner."

Outside, Vanessa looked at the clouds. They were dark and menacing. Lightning streaked through them, producing a low rumbling over the city noise. "Rain," she said, pointing toward the gray veils that obscured the horizon.

"We had better get back to the ranch."

"We could spend the night at your place," she suggested. "It's closer."

"No," he said.

She leaned toward him and gazed into his eyes. "Why?"

"Because I don't want the memories of you there," he stated bluntly.

"After we go our separate ways."

"That's right."

His tone was harsh, unrelenting. She sighed. Like this case, he considered her a temporary assignment in his life. "Okay," she said softly.

He gave her a surprised glance. "No argument?"

"I don't feel up to it."

"Good." He opened the door to the SUV and helped her up with a hand under her elbow. "Dinner before we go back?" he asked when he was inside.

"The storm might break before we get home."

"I'm not afraid of the rain."

"I am. I might melt if I get wet." She injected teasing laughter into her voice.

"You're not that sweet," he replied dryly.

She leaned close and breathed in his ear, "That's not what you said last night."

His ears turned somewhat pink. "A man says fool things at crucial times."

Satisfied at getting back at him for refusing to take her to his home, she fastened the seat belt and watched the familiar scenery glide by on the trip back to the ranch.

The sky turned completely dark, hiding the twilight glow of the city as they headed out the county road. The lights of the truck cast black shadows into the ravine beside the road as the oaks and willows writhed with the moaning of the rising wind.

A funny sensation crawled along her back between her shoulder blades.

"Damn," Dev said.

At the same moment she heard a crack like thunder, then the truck veered sharply left, sending their rear wheels into a skid…straight toward the ravine.

Dev cut the wheel left, but the truck wouldn't obey. Instead it wobbled eerily as it continued to slide toward the drop-off into darkness. She heard a loud crack as they swiped a thin sapling. The tree hit her side of the vehicle and broke in two, its top part sliding over the hood with a scratching sound.

"Dev?" she said, not sure what was happening.

Her head careened into the window as they tilted wildly. Points of light shattered behind her eyelids. She felt herself sliding into the darkness of the ravine, only it seemed to be inside her now.

"We're going over the side," Dev said grimly.

She forced her eyes open and saw him battling the wheel. He worked with the gear lever and used one foot on the brake, the other on the accelerator. She frowned as dizziness washed over her. She should tell him that he couldn't brake and speed up at the same time.

There was another loud crackling, then they came to a dead stop. She stared at the tree that blocked her window, which was now cracked into a million tiny fragments but still of a piece.

"What happened?" she asked in the silence.

"Someone shot out the tire," Dev said in a tight voice.

Ten

Dev pulled the cell phone from his pocket and punched in Wyatt's number. The sheriff was still at his desk. Dev explained the situation.

"Sit tight. I'll have a crew out there at once."

"I think I can get us on the road," Dev told him. "I'd like a cast of any tire tracks you find on the road that leads up to the hill above us. I want to see how they compare to those you found on the bootmaker's road."

"Will do."

Dev hung up. "Okay, hold on. I think this junk heap will pull us out of here."

"Okay."

He gazed at her in the dim glow of the dash lights. "You're a brave woman," he murmured, then turned his attention to their predicament.

The front wheels were still on the shoulder of the road. Keeping one foot ready on the brake, he changed to first gear in four-wheel drive and pressed lightly on the gas pedal. The truck shuddered, then began to move. He kept his touch on the accelerator light and steady. Slowly the truck inched forward, the tree that had stopped their skid gouging the paint along the passenger side as they moved.

At last they were on the road.

Dev got out and set about changing the flat. "That's one tire I won't have to worry about changing again," he remarked, jovial now that the danger was behind them.

"Someone wanted to hurt us," she said slowly, looking up at the trees on the hill above the road. "How do you know he's gone?"

"No one is shooting at us."

He checked her over, noting the steadiness of her hands as she smoothed her hair from her face. She was all right. He stored the ruined tire in the truck. The deputies arrived just as he finished.

"I'm going up the hill," he told Vanessa. "You can stay in the truck. It's going to rain soon."

"I'm coming with you."

He recognized the determined tone and didn't argue. The two of them and a deputy hiked up the steep incline. With a powerful flashlight, the deputy found the footprints where the shooter had stood. There was no casing. The man had been careful to leave nothing with fingerprints. But he had left a set of tire tracks in the dust.

The deputy called his partner on the radio. They got a set of tracks in plaster before the first drops of rain fell. Dev took Vanessa by the hand and ran for the truck. They made it just as the deluge began.

Arriving at the hacienda a short time later, they dashed to the side door and into their rooms.

"Your poor truck," she murmured.

He grinned. "It did its job."

"And that's all you expect from it," she concluded. She sighed. "Being frightened is very tiring."

Dev stopped her at the adjoining door. He examined her face and delved into her eyes. She was more than tired. The vulnerable sadness was back. He enfolded her in his arms.

"We're beginning to get somewhere," he assured her, kissing the top of her head. "They're warning us to back off. That means they think we're getting too close."

"I wish," she said, her face buried in his shirt.

For a long while neither said anything. He could feel her heart beat against him, feel the warmth of her breath through his clothing. He nuzzled her temple. Somewhere in him, a little-used, creaky, rusty door opened slowly and reluctantly. Like a sudden light shining in the eyes, he felt a painful contraction in that secret place.

He could no more shut her out than he could stop the rain from falling. It pelted the roof and windows now in a steady roar. And he admitted he was lost to reason.

"Come to bed," he coaxed. "Things will look brighter in the morning."

She nodded.

He helped her undress, then tucked her under the sheet. He joined her in another moment, pulling her close to warm her when he felt the coldness of her hands and feet.

"Until the kidnapping, I'd never realized exactly how cruel the world could be."

"I know, Beauty, I know," he murmured, soothing her as best he could. He held her until she relaxed into sleep. For a long time he lay awake, savoring the pleasure of her closeness. But he already felt the emptiness that would come when they parted.

* * *

Dev woke just as the sun broke over the horizon and lit the window of his room. Vanessa nestled against him, her arm and leg thrown across him. A soft knock on the door caused every nerve in his body to tighten.

"Yeah?" he called softly.

Ryan Fortune stuck his head in the door. His keen gaze took in the situation at a glance, then he stared directly at Dev. Dev stared back, refusing to blink or explain her presence or even to jog her awake.

"A meeting in an hour in my office," Ryan said quietly. "Can you make it?"

Dev nodded. His lover's father stepped back and closed the door. Dev wondered what other interesting things fate had in store for him. "Hey, time to wake up."

When he explained about the meeting, she sat up. "We'd better get ready. I'm going, too."

He nodded at her defiant glance. "I figured you would."

They showered and dressed and ate a muffin before heading for the master suite and the office. Ryan was at the desk when they entered.

Vanessa went to her father and dropped a kiss on his cheek. "Is there news?" she asked.

"You probably know that better than I do," he replied ruefully, glancing over her shoulder at Dev. "I felt like a meeting was in order to go over things. Especially the information on the tracks Wyatt found at the scene of the shooting, which he told me about this morning. You could have mentioned that last night."

"It was late when we arrived. I didn't want to wake you in case you'd already gone to bed."

"Huh," her father said.

Dev took up a position opposite the door and observed each man as he appeared. The sheriff arrived on Matthew's heels. Sam Waterman was last. Ryan greeted each man, then closed the door after Waterman.

Before he could take the seat behind the desk again, the door opened. Clint Lockhart stood in the doorway. "I understand there's a meeting about the kidnapping. Okay if I sit in?"

Dev didn't miss the frown that flitted ever so briefly across Ryan's face before he nodded and told his brother-in-law to join them. They went through the ritual of serving coffee before Ryan got down to business.

"Wyatt, you want to go first?" the patriarch invited.

The sheriff nodded and took out a notebook. He flipped it open. "The truck that followed Kincaid and Vanessa to the Tomahawks' home was the same one on the hill where they were shot at."

"Shot at!" Clint looked stunned.

"They aimed for the tire," Dev said dryly.

"And hit it," Wyatt continued. "The handwriting samples are the same. We have a name, too. Jack Mason. Drifter. Rodeo bum. Cowboy when he runs out of money. According to his sister in Amarillo, he's always trying to find a get-rich-quick scheme. He has a record, so we got fingerprints on him."

Dev surveyed the group when Wyatt paused. Matthew looked haggard and dispirited. Sam was tight-lipped, his eyes angry, his manner controlled. Clint, after that first exclamation, revealed nothing, his face as impassive as a plaster of Paris mask.

"Mason is our man," Wyatt said. "It was his print at the hotel and on the rowel. He's the kidnapper."

"Have you picked him up?" Sam demanded.

"That's the problem. We don't know where he is. He appears, then disappears just as quickly. I figure he has a bolt-hole in San Antonio. We have a bulletin out to report his whereabouts but not to engage him if he's spotted again."

"We need to be careful," Sam warned. "If he panics, he may shoot everything in sight—"

"Including my son," Matthew broke in.

Dev knew Sam was speaking from his experience in dealing with terrorists. Their behavior was predictable. Desperate men were the same the world over.

"The FBI has jurisdiction," he said. He looked directly at Wyatt. "All action is to be coordinated through me. You have my cell phone number. Use it."

Wyatt nodded curtly.

Dev looked at Sam.

The private detective nodded, then added, "I'll make sure McCoy has your number, too."

"He does." Dev looked at Ryan, then Clint. "I don't suppose I have to remind you how important it is that this information remain among this group only." He glanced at Matthew. "Not even wives."

"What about lovers?" Clint drawled, his glance going deliberately to his niece.

Dev didn't take the bait. "Not even lovers," he said, staring directly into the man's eyes, telling

Lockhart he knew exactly who his lovers were, until the man dropped his arrogant gaze. "When we find where the man and his accomplice are holed up, I'll take a special team in to arrest them. Anyone moves on this without my okay is going to be hauled up on federal charges for interfering in an investigation."

Vanessa, putting away her personal concerns, watched the interaction between the men with professional interest. Dev had been speaking to her uncle and brother. He didn't consider Wyatt, Sam, or her father, a problem.

He also didn't care for Uncle Clint, although there was nothing specific in his demeanor to indicate this. It was intuitive knowledge on her part.

The way she knew she and Dev were meant for each other.

She caught her father's eyes on her. He studied her intently, unaware of her gaze on him, his manner troubled. When he caught her eye, he smiled as if to reassure her that all would be well. She managed a small upturn of her lips.

She stayed silent as the men talked, then Dev dismissed them with a reminder to report any findings to him.

When they left, Dev turned to her father. "I don't think it will be long now," he said.

"Until you catch the kidnappers?" she asked.

His dark blue gaze fell on her. "Until we hear something, one way or another."

A chill rushed over her. Someone walking over her grave, Rosita would have said. She hugged her arms across her chest. "It can't be soon enough for me."

"Nor for me," her father agreed.

Her heart went out to him. He looked so tired. She had learned with her mother's death that her father didn't command the fates, but she had still thought of him as next to God in power. Now she knew him to be a vulnerable man.

Dev dropped an arm across her shoulders, surprising her with the show of affection. "It'll be all right," he promised softly. "We'll get Bryan back."

She could only gaze at him with her heart in her eyes while love clutched at her chest, making her ache for all the joy she was afraid they were going to miss.

"I know. But be careful. I don't want you hurt. Promise me you'll be careful."

"I'm always careful," he stated.

Her father cleared his throat. "You'll keep me informed of any developments?"

"Of course, sir," Dev replied in his polite way.

"A black pickup with a hitch on the back," Wyatt told them Thursday afternoon. "The sister described the truck."

Vanessa looked at Dev. "That's about half the pickups in the state of Texas."

"Well, it rules out the other half."

"The license plate is stolen. He's probably changed it again by now." Wyatt laid the report aside.

"Yeah," Dev agreed, "but he used the same truck at the motel as at the ranch. He's got new tires whose tread shows up nicely in the dust. He left a date and the name of the paper in the ransom note and the newspaper scraps at the motel. All mistakes. He's made others. Our job is to find the one that leads us to him."

Vanessa experienced the familiar clutching in her chest while she watched her love sort through their meager evidence. Thorough and polite, he continued in the face of every obstacle.

She had trailed along with him and Wyatt as they went over the shooting scene again that afternoon in case the deputies had missed something the night before. The rain had washed out all traces of the incident, except for the broken sapling and the missing bark from the larger tree.

A near tragedy. She or Dev could have been killed. The terrible ache of love invaded her. If he had died, how could she bear it? It came to her that if she had died, Dev would never forgive himself.

In that instant she knew because of their involvement he would never love again if something happened to her. He would never trust life or have faith in himself that he could protect the ones he loved.

And that would be an even worse tragedy. He was one of the most honorable men she had ever known, true and brave and fine. He would be a wonderful husband and father.

Oh, love, love…

Staring at the calendar on Wyatt's wall, she realized that as of today, she had known Dev two weeks. An eternity.

"Ready?"

She glanced up into his eyes, confused by the question. She realized he was standing. "Yes. Thank you, Wyatt, for all your help," she said sincerely.

Outside the sheriff's office, she and Dev watched the busy traffic along the street for a minute.

"You're quiet," he remarked.

His plangent voice reminded her of peaceful waves breaking on a moon-washed beach. She swallowed against the longing that rose, all hot and swift and purposeful, in her. "I was thinking about children," she said.

The guarded look came into his beautiful desolate eyes. Beyond it, she saw a need that he wouldn't recognize but she knew to be the same as her own—the need to belong, to establish a home and raise a family.

"We'd better go," he said.

She refused to let him off so easily. "I want children, Dev. I want them to be yours. Ours."

He shook his head, a quick, angry gesture. But in his eyes she saw the tortured longing he wouldn't acknowledge.

"Women always get nesty," he advised, taking a sardonic approach. "You'll get over it."

"Will you?" she asked softly.

He ignored the question. "It's after five. Are you ready for dinner?"

"Yes. We forgot to eat lunch."

He drove them to a quiet place away from the Alamo and its busy churning of humanity. The restaurant was small, elegant and reclusive. He was greeted warmly by the hostess.

"The place is family owned," he explained after they were seated and had been served long-stemmed goblets of wine. "They've been here almost as long as your family."

He consulted with the chef, who came to their table to tell them the day's specials, and suggested she might like a chicken dish served with rice.

After their order was complete, she studied him. "You come here often?"

"Often enough."

"I'm trying to decide if I'm jealous."

Dev found the idea preposterous. "Why should you be?"

"You're friendly and glad to be here. You enjoyed talking with the chef. You make them welcome in your life."

"But not you?"

"Not our love."

The futility of it swamped him. He didn't know how to convince her that what she wanted just wasn't possible. He couldn't promise forever when he had no idea if tomorrow even existed.

"I warned you," he told her. "Don't expect anything. That way, life is full of surprises."

Her springtime eyes filled with pain. "Be kind," she suddenly requested. "For tonight, let me dream."

Her words almost unmanned him. He tasted each separate pain of loving her, one bitter pill at a time as it lodged in his throat. "All right," he said, his voice husky with the impossible need to give her everything she thought she wanted from him.

After the meal, he took her dancing.

"Our first dance," she said, her eyes aglow, filled with fox fire, with magic.

For him, all for him.

The most magical of all was that she thought it was real. For tonight, so would he.

She had dressed in her green silk outfit for the trip to town after searching the hill for clues. The silk was smooth and cool to his touch. Under it, her flesh was as smooth, but she was warm, a magical being of promise and passion. For him.

The ache of hunger ran deep within his body, matching the pain of longing he'd experienced as a boy when he'd thought by wishing hard enough he could make it happen.

But neither his wishes nor his mother's prayers had been enough.

The green-eyed woman in his arms didn't know that yet. She believed…and, God help him, he couldn't crush her dreams under his heel as if they didn't matter.

The hours passed, but still he held her. They danced slow and fast tunes. They laughed. He bought her a kir royale and an Irish coffee for himself.

"That's the first time I've seen you drink anything alcoholic," she murmured.

"This is my only tipple," he admitted. "It's good for a cold winter's night."

"This is August in Texas."

"Yeah, heat and humidity."

She wrinkled her nose at him, playful and smiling. He wanted to lean across the table and gather her into his arms for a long, long kiss.

His eyes must have conveyed his thoughts for her breath caught, then escaped between her parted lips. Her eyes darkened to smoky emerald while his blood ran thick and hot and urgent in him.

Words rushed to his tongue. Foolish words. He held them inside with an effort. Words signified nothing. Like the promises they made, they weren't meant for believing.

Her lips formed themselves into a silent message. *I love you.*

He shook his head while darkness ate at him.

I love you. Insistent. Stubborn. Proud.

Hope and despair warred for his soul. Forcing a smile, he lifted her hand to his lips. "It's midnight, Cinderella. Let's go home before you find out the prince is a frog."

"My prince is a knight," she murmured.

She spoke so softly, he hardly heard the words with his ears. It was his heart that was hearing things now.

He paid the check and led her outside. Once in the battered truck, he cranked up and turned toward the suburbs of town. She didn't ask about their destination, but sat there silent and watchful until he turned in his drive.

"Your house?" she finally asked.

"Yes."

The word came out gruff, defensive. He leaned across and opened her door, then climbed out. She was standing on the drive when he came around the truck.

At his door, she hesitated, her eyes on his, open and honest in her reactions. "Memories," she reminded him.

"They're already inside." He tapped his chest.

Her lips trembled. A hundred emotions flashed in her eyes before she stepped into the house. He followed, knowing he would pay for this night. And the price would be high.

The streetlight cast a glow over the silent rooms. He took her hand and led the way to the bedroom.

Damn the price. He would have this night and the memories.

Taking her face between his hands, he gazed into her eyes, which were filled with wonder. An ache hit him. She was the sun, casting her radiance into the darkness that lived within him. He kissed her. She opened for him and let him take her sweetness until his knees grew weak.

At last he took her to his bed. There, in the spill of moonlight across the sheet, he made love to her, giving her anything she wanted from him…his body…his heart…his desperate hope for the future.

"Love, love," she murmured, filling him with her splendor until he almost believed it was all possible.

Clint Lockhart quietly closed the door to the pickup, an action far from what he actually felt. He went in the front door of the bar in the strip mall. After ordering a beer, then taking the bottle with him, he went down the back hall toward the men's room. Instead of using it, he went on out the back door and into the night.

He moved through the dark with quick, angry strides, his feet sure on the track he had followed to meet the beauteous Sophia many times over the years. At first it had amused him to toy with the wife of his brother-in-law. But now, the situation had become more complicated than simple sex.

He knocked on the door of the end room at the Moonlight Motel. It opened at once. He stepped inside and closed the door behind him.

"Did anyone follow you?" Sophia asked, her

beautifully made-up face showing signs of strain as the past few weeks weighed on her.

"No."

"You're sure?" She risked a peek out the dusty metal blinds. "It's quiet tonight. I don't like it."

"It's Thursday. What do you expect?"

"That's right. No cowboys or ranchers out on the town." She yanked the drapes over the blinds and made sure the centers met so that no one could look in.

"Why all the caution?" he asked sarcastically. "That stupid cowboy you hired has already messed up but good."

She raised her carefully shaped eyebrows in question.

"The fool shot out the tire on the FBI agent's truck." Clint gave in to anger and kicked the rickety chair out of the way as he paced the length of the room.

"It was a warning—"

"It was a damn dumb idea. Whose was it— yours?" He spun and glared at Sophia, who gave him one of her wide-eyed innocent looks as she settled on the side of the bed. Her skirt slipped up her thigh.

She kicked her heels off and lay back on the floral bedspread, her breasts high and tight against her blouse. "Of course not, darling. He thought the FBI was getting too close. He wanted to warn Ryan about what would happen if he didn't cooperate."

Clint stuck his hands on his hips. "Yeah? Is that a fact? What about the plan to lay low until the FBI agent packed up his toys and went home? You think he's going to clear out with somebody shooting at him? He had Vanessa in the truck with him at the time. Ryan is fit to be tied."

She shrugged. "Let him stew. It'll make him more willing to pay up when we contact him again."

Clint cursed in frustration. "You don't get it. Overplay our hand, and we'll all end up in the slammer."

Smiling, she ran her hand down her side. "Are we going to argue all night?" Her eyes issued a blatant invitation.

He stopped and stared down at her lithe form curled sexily on the bed. She rubbed the inside of his leg with one delicate foot.

"All right," he said, "here's what we do. We make our move on Monday. Ryan can get the money out of the bank that afternoon and deliver it at dusk. That cowboy and his friend had better handle this right. Tell 'em to get gassed up and stock up an extra couple of five-gallon cans for the getaway. They'll need food and water to hole up in the desert for two weeks. After that, we wait two months before meeting and splitting the ransom."

"What about the FBI?"

"You think he's going to leave now? Fat chance. We'll have to work around him...or through him if he gets in the way." His laughter was brief and harsh. "He won't. He's fallen for the daughter of the house."

Sophia rose and ran her hands over his lean, tough torso. "Mmm, I love the feel of a hard, strong body."

He grabbed a handful of blond hair and hauled her head back. "You understand what you're supposed to do?"

Anger flashed in her eyes, then was gone. She nodded. He let her go.

"I've waited a long time for this," he muttered. "Nothing is going to stand in my way, not the FBI, not the sheriff..." He smiled down at her. "Not even you, honey."

She pouted at him. "We're on the same side. We both want Ryan Fortune to pay. He will. Lots. He's vulnerable where his precious offspring are concerned. He'll pay to get his grandson back. I wish I could see him now."

Clint laughed and threw himself down on the bed beside her. "Miserable bastard. Between the kidnapping and the divorce, we got him by the short hairs. He'll do exactly what we tell him...or else."

She laughed as she leaned over him. Her lips were warm and sweet. He forgot his anger.

Eleven

Vanessa woke and reached across the bed. It was empty. She yawned and opened her eyes to the new day, then glanced at the window of her room. From the brightness outside, she judged the sun to have been up for some time.

She and Dev had spent Friday, Saturday, and most of yesterday at his house in San Antonio. They had gone for long walks, had cooked all their own meals and shared every moment with each other, savoring each one.

As if it might be the last.

She had seen that in his eyes. Pulling her knees to her chest, she sighed contentedly. They now had the memory of one wonderful weekend to carry inside them the rest of their lives. A sweet, warm memory of perfect happiness.

Today was Monday. Time to get back to reality. Dev was probably meeting with her father. Rising, she showered, then dressed in tan jeans with a green and tan striped blouse. She slipped a green stretchy band over her head to hold her hair out of her face.

After selecting a muffin and orange juice from the sideboard in the breakfast room, she hurried to the office.

"Come in," her father said when she knocked.

She was glad to see Lily inside when she entered. Dev stood at the window overlooking the inner courtyard, a mug of coffee in his hand. He nodded when she glanced his way.

"How are you?" she said warmly to the other female.

She felt a rush of emotion for her father and his fiancée, for all those years they had spent apart and the complications of the divorce that plagued them now. Lily surely became discouraged at times, but she was always calm and cheerful around the family.

"I'm fine," Lily replied. "You look especially lovely this morning." Her eyes twinkled, and her tone was affectionate and approving as she spoke.

"Thank you." Warmth flooded Vanessa's heart and reached her face. She tried to tamp the glow into submission, but it bubbled inside her like the spring that fed the fountain.

Lily's smile widened. Vanessa felt as if they shared a wonderful secret.

Dev looked on, his eyes gathering her in until she felt his perusal as a caress. Unable to stay away from him another second, she crossed the room and kissed his cheek. He didn't move a muscle, but the pupils of his eyes widened and a faint flush spread lightly over his face.

She refrained from laughing. He was never quite sure how to handle her love for him, and she wasn't going to hide it just to spare his blushes.

"Please. Don't let me interrupt," she requested. She chose a seat close to her love and started on her breakfast.

"I was explaining," her father said, bringing her

into the conversation, "that the ransom money is available. The bank has agreed to furnish the bills in twenties, fifties, or hundreds, whatever the kidnappers want, given an hour's notice."

Dev snorted. "I hope the perps realize how large a package fifty million dollars is in twenty-dollar bills."

"Two point five million individual bills," Ryan said, his mouth thin with anger. "A half million, if they'll take it in hundred dollar denominations."

"It'll take a couple of large duffel bags." Dev refilled his mug.

"I'm going into town," Ryan informed them. "Lily has some work to do. I have a lunch appointment with my son at one. I'll probably stay in town tonight."

"You'll have your cell phone with you?" Dev asked.

"Yes. And I have your number if anything comes up."

Her father came around the desk and stopped in front of them. To her surprise, he bent and took her face in his gentle clasp. As a child, she'd thought he had the biggest, strongest hands of anyone in the entire world.

Tears stung her eyes and nose when he kissed her on the forehead. "Take care," he murmured, a world of love in his eyes. He ushered Lily out.

Silence filled the room. She managed a catchy little laugh. "Sometimes I forget how much I love my father."

"And how much he loves you?"

She nodded and blinked the moisture from her

eyes. Dev ran a finger along her eyelashes on one side. Her heart squeezed into a knot at the look in his eyes.

He hadn't repeated the magical words of love to her, but in his eyes…oh, there was tenderness and caring and such terrible yearning. He fought showing his feelings, but love was reflected in his every touch, every glance, in his gentleness and his vast patience with her.

"How I wish I could show you my heart," she whispered.

"Would it be the heart of a coquette?" he teased, now shielding his thoughts behind the curtain of restraint.

"Did you read that story?"

"A long time ago."

"At the center of her heart was the image of the man she had loved all those years." She touched his brow. "Just as you are the center of mine."

The door opened at that moment. Matthew strode in. "I have to be at the hospital in an hour. I'm thinking of moving back to the house in town to be closer to my patients. What do you think?"

Vanessa sized up her brother. He was agitated, a faint flush of anger on his cheeks, his mouth crimped at the corners as if he held in a torrent of emotion. Another quarrel with Claudia?

"I don't see a problem," Dev told him. "We have all the phones covered in case of a call."

Matthew hesitated, looked from one to the other, then nodded and walked out.

"He's so desperately unhappy," she murmured, worry eating at her as they listened to the sound of her brother's footsteps recede, then the slam of the front door.

"It's a hard situation for a parent."

"For all of us." She sighed and finished off the juice. "What are you going to do today?"

He shook his head. "We've followed every lead we have. Now we wait. The kidnappers will contact us soon. They're growing impatient."

She visibly jumped when the phone rang. Dev motioned for her to get it. "Hello?" Her voice trembled.

"Vanessa? This is Sophia. Is your father there?"

"No, he's on his way to town. To see his attorney," she added, then was ashamed of the barb. *Sophia,* she mouthed to Dev. He whipped out his cell phone and punched in a number.

Sophia paused. "I don't suppose you've heard anything on the kidnapping?"

"No."

"I know we haven't been close, but I am sorry about this. It must be terrible on the family."

"Yes, terrible," she agreed, and wondered why her stepmother had really called.

"Is the FBI agent still in residence?"

Vanessa paused. "He's here in the office. Do you wish to speak to him?"

"Uh, no. I just wondered if anything…well, I'm sure it would be on the news if anything had happened."

"Keep her talking," Dev murmured. He spoke into the cell phone in a low tense tone.

Surprised, Vanessa cleared her throat and asked, "How are you doing?"

"Oh, I'm fine. Well, I should go—"

"Has there been any action on the farm bill there in Austin? You are in Austin, aren't you?"

"Uh, yes, at the Austin Arms, of course. I have a hair appointment. I must run. Give my best to your father." She hung up.

Vanessa put her hand over the receiver and looked a question at Dev. He held up a finger, signaling for her to wait a minute.

"Okay," he said into the phone, then looked at her. "Okay, hang up."

She did so and watched him, perplexed.

"Where did she say she was?" he asked.

"In Austin."

He shook his head. "She's in San Antonio, but we couldn't make the trace to the actual phone. We know what exchange she was using, though."

"She has a room at the Palace Lights in San Antonio."

He relayed that information via his phone. "Right. Okay, thanks for trying." He hung up. "She wasn't in that area, either."

"She was fishing for information on my dad. She's done that before, especially when she thinks Lily is with him. It's odd. She's unfaithful, but she goes into a rage if he sees another woman."

"Perhaps she doesn't like the competition," Dev suggested.

She nodded absently. "I probably should work with the stallion before he forgets all Cruz and I have taught him."

"Go ahead. I'll stay here in case there's a call."

When she hesitated, Dev took her by the shoulders and pointed her toward the door.

"Get some fresh air," he advised. He kissed her in the vicinity of her ear. "I've got papers to go over."

She wondered about his other case but didn't ask. If she asked, he would tell her, but he wouldn't volunteer information. In time, he would come to trust her. For a second she wondered how much time she had…

He hooked a finger under her chin and kissed her on the lips. She clung to him for a minute, then left.

At the stables, she found Cruz in the office. He was on the phone with the supplier of minerals and vitamins for the horses. "No, no additives, no hormones. You know how the Double Crown feels about that."

She smiled at the way all of them referred to the ranch as if it were a person.

"Wait a minute, I need a piece of paper." Cruz glanced around the desk surface, which was cluttered with catalogs of every sort a rancher might need.

She spotted a notepad on the floor behind the desk, mostly hidden behind the thick wooden leg. Dropping to her knees, she reached under the old oak desk that had belonged to her grandfather, Kingston Fortune, and retrieved the pad. She tossed it to the desk, but Cruz had already written the information from the supplier on the margin of a catalog.

"Okay, I'll get back to you," he said, and hung up. "Why can't suppliers deliver what they're supposed to deliver on the day they promised to deliver it?" he growled.

Vanessa shrugged. "I'm going to work in the ring for a while with the black. Anything else we need to do?"

"No."

She collected her tack and saddled up the stallion. He shook his head, ready for a run. "Not today," she soothed. "It's time you learned to curb that impatience and do the work asked of you." She led him into the ring.

Within ten minutes, the stallion settled down and followed each command she gave with a willingness that pleased her. If only certain other males would be as willing…

She smiled at the thought of Dev obeying a bit and bridle. He'd put anyone straight who tried to rope him in. Still smiling she took the black out into the pasture for a good run before they ended the session.

Dev was still in the office when Rosita came in. "I have the mail," she said.

A premonition stiffened the hair on his neck. Rosita usually deposited the family mail on a table in the great room and gave the business mail to her husband or son to take down to the ranch office.

"There is something here…" Her voice trailed off in uncertainty.

"Let me see," he instructed, holding out his hand.

He saw at once that the letter had no postmark. Someone had personally delivered it to the mailbox located where the ranch road met the county road. The second thing he noticed was that the envelope contained a single name—Ryan Fortune—and that the letters had been cut from a newspaper.

Well, the kidnappers were consistent.

"Thanks. I'll handle it," he said to the housekeeper, his heart kicking up a bit.

"This is bad," she said. "I feel the energy. It is

from anger.'' With a worried frown, she left the room, closing the door silently.

Since it was practically impossible to lift a clear set of prints from well-handled porous material, Dev wasn't too worried about contamination as he slit open the envelope. Inside there was a single sheet of paper wrapped around a blurred photo of a baby. He dropped the contents onto another sheet of paper without touching the photograph, knowing the glossy-coated film paper might prove more promising when it came to lifting prints. He doubted it would disclose any, though. The perps were sharper than that.

The message was brief. It advised they would receive a call this evening telling them where to drop the money and pick up the child. They would speak only to Ryan Fortune. He was to have the money ready when they called.

Dev wasn't surprised that the patriarch of the clan was the man the perps would contact. They obviously knew who controlled the purse strings. More than that was Dev's gut feeling that a great part of this case was revenge on Ryan.

By Sophia Fortune, who had no inclination to be faithful to her husband, but wanted all the perks and money the Fortunes commanded?

By Clint Lockhart, who harbored a childhood grudge against Ryan for being more successful than his own father?

By Cruz Perez, who was saving nearly every penny he made for the day he could buy his own place to get out from under the Fortune shadow?

By Ruben Perez, who, to all appearances, was a loyal ranch manager?

By one of Lily Cassidy's kids? One who might resent their mother's involvement with Ryan, who couldn't seem to wrangle a divorce from his present wife?

By Lily herself, who might have gotten tired of being strung along and decided to go for the money?

By any of the dozens of friends and neighbors and business associates of the Fortune family, or ranch, or even Fortune TX, Ltd., their business holdings?

And then there were the Fortune heirs from either Ryan's or Cameron's side of the family. Someone who maybe wanted to secure their inheritance before it was due. Cameron's oldest son Holden had a wild past, while Dallas was a moody recluse. Logan and Zane were the second born in their respective families. Perhaps one of them felt resentment at being overshadowed by the oldest sons and the younger kids.

He ruled out the girls—Cameron's daughter Eden and Ryan's twins Vanessa and Victoria—simply because they either hadn't been present or were accounted for.

Picking up the cell phone, he called Ryan. "We've had a message."

"What do I have to do?"

He gave the older man credit for control. His tone had been tense but calm and composed. In a battle, Dev would like to have Ryan at his side.

"Get back to the ranch sometime this afternoon. They're going to call and give instructions this evening at some unspecified time."

"Okay. Should I alert my banker?"

"I would, sir."

"Should I bring the money with me?"

"Yes. The drop-off will most likely be today or in the morning." He hesitated. "Or they may send you someplace to pick up further instructions. Some people like to play games."

"Especially these. They want to see me suffer."

"Vanessa thinks so, too. I agree."

Ryan sighed. "It makes a man wonder what terrible sin he committed that another person would want to punish him like this—through a child…an innocent child."

Dev had no comforting words to offer.

"I'll be home by three. It will take that long for me to get the money and get it signed for. If you need me before then, let me know."

"I will." Dev said goodbye and hung up.

A sense of melancholy seeped into his spirits like ink through a blotter. He had always had the ability to separate the needs of his job from the needs of the victims. He knew and understood grief, and he'd never let feelings get in the way of his duty.

He wouldn't now.

Yet he felt a deep sorrow for Ryan Fortune. The man had had some good fortune—so had his father, who had married the original owner of the land—but they had also worked hard and made wise decisions where other ranchers suffering the same weather and market conditions had failed.

Fate had conspired to rob Ryan Fortune of peace of mind at a stage of his life where he should be able to kick back and relax a little, to enjoy the resurrection of his first love and the birth of his first grandchild.

He carefully put the items back in the envelope and slipped them into a larger one. He had time to run to town to get the lab to check the photo for whatever it might tell them.

Once in his truck, he started the engine, then sat there in indecision. He muttered an expletive, put the SUV into gear and drove to the stables.

The stallion was in the pasture. He checked the tack room. Not there. Passing by the office, he heard laughter and veered toward the door.

Vanessa was inside, sitting on the corner of an old massive desk. Cruz and his father were with her. Through the dusty window, they looked like a happy group. They were completely at ease with each other. Cruz sat at the desk, his arm near Vanessa's thigh. Irritation twanged through Dev, surprising him. He recognized the emotion for what it really was—jealousy of the younger man's closeness to her and of her loyalty to her childhood friend.

Someday she would marry a man like that; one who could share her dreams. A young man who had hopes of his own.

Dev stood outside until the older man finished a story about trying to keep a determined armadillo out of Rosita's kitchen garden when they were young and first married. He knocked once and opened the door.

An instant silence fell on the room.

He nodded to the men, then looked at Vanessa. "I have to go to town. I, uh, thought you might like to ride along."

His ears felt hot long before he got to the end of the sentence, which seemed way too complicated for a simple suggestion.

Her smile blinded him with its brilliance. "Yes. I'll see you later," she said to the other two, then she came to him. Outside, she linked her arm with his. "Do I have time to change clothes? I've been working with the black this morning."

"No, I'm in a hurry."

The shine left her face. "What is it?" she asked.

"We've had news. The kidnappers will contact your father with instructions tonight. I want to have Charlie at the lab check the letter before then."

She climbed into the truck without another word. Worry shadowed her eyes. Her mouth looked soft, vulnerable. "Did they say anything about Bryan?"

"They sent a Polaroid print. I want it checked by the lab before anyone handles it," he added.

"Oh, yes. Of course. Matthew and Claudia will want to see it, naturally. And my father." She hesitated. "Do you think Bryan is okay?"

"As far as one can tell from a snapshot."

Charlie was at the lab, eating lunch and studying a report. "I'm not moving until I finish my meal," he announced as soon as he saw Dev come through the door.

"Okay." Dev removed the envelope from his pocket and laid it in the middle of the cluttered desk in the crime lab. He pulled up two stools for him and Vanessa at the lab table where Charlie sat.

Charlie eyed the envelope. "What is it?"

"A letter."

"Oh." He went back to his report.

"And a photo."

Charlie glanced at Dev suspiciously. Dev gazed out

the window at the traffic. "What kind of photo?" Charlie asked.

"Of the Fortune baby."

Charlie looked aggrieved. "Why didn't you say so?" He jumped off the stool and retrieved the letter after pulling on gloves. He dusted the photo. "No prints."

"Can you tell me anything about when the photo was taken?"

Charlie was busy setting out a flat, shallow pan and a tray of chemicals. He scanned the photo into the computer, then rubbed the corner. "The date indicates the picture was taken yesterday. Of course, that can be set at any day you want. However, the photo is fresh, not more than twenty-four hours old, I'd say."

"That's what I thought, too," Dev said in his serious, contemplative manner.

Vanessa peered over the lab man's shoulder. Her heart caught in her throat. "He looks okay. He's gained weight."

Charlie stepped back and let her get a closer look.

"His face is rounder, fuller." She pressed a hand to her breast. "They grow so fast at this age."

Dev came to her and slipped a hand around her waist, holding her close, sensing her need for comfort. "Tomorrow," he murmured. "We'll get him back tomorrow."

She laid her head against his shoulder. "I hope so. I have just about given up hope."

He squeezed her, then stepped back. "Let's go to lunch and let Charlie get on with his work. We'll be back in an hour or so," he said to the other man.

Charlie nodded, already busy on the photo.

"I want to check in with your father," Dev said once they were in the SUV. He called Ryan, who invited them to join him at the offices of Fortune TX, Ltd. Ryan was about to have lunch with his son Zane, Executive Director of Marketing. The bank president would deliver the money personally.

The secretary showed them in when they arrived. Vanessa kissed her brother, then her father in greeting. Dev shook hands with the men.

"Lunch is ready," Zane announced. "We'll use the conference room."

Her brother was dressed in a blue summer suit that enhanced his sun-streaked blond, blue-eyed good looks. She and Victoria thought he should have gone to Hollywood and become a star instead of staying in Texas and becoming a business tycoon. But he seemed to like his job…and the social life of the city, if the gossip columns were to be believed. And they were.

His expression was quiet, serious and threaded with subdued anger, the same as Dallas's when he spoke of the kidnapping.

They served themselves from a trolley loaded with Tex-Mex dishes—tortilla soup, chicken breasts that had been flattened, battered and fried to a golden brown, broccoli slaw, chips made from colored corn-meal and served with fresh guacamole dip.

"Have you heard anything else?" her father demanded as soon as the heavy door closed behind him.

"No. The lab checked the photo. There were no fingerprints. I didn't expect any."

"They're careful," Zane said, an expression of pure rage crossing his handsome features.

"But they've made mistakes. They'll make others." Vanessa turned to Dev. "Matthew and Claudia will want to see the picture. Do you think we can take it with us?"

"Charlie can make us a copy. He'll take out the light glare. It'll be clearer."

"It's hard, this waiting," Ryan said.

She gave her father a sympathetic pat on the shoulder before bending over her soup. Dev sat beside her while Zane had taken the other side. Her father sat at the end of the shining walnut table.

"I saw Parker Malone this morning," Ryan mentioned.

"The divorce lawyer," Vanessa reminded Dev. She knew he had talked to the attorney, who had also been present at the christening party.

"He's going to petition the court for the final decree on the divorce. The settlement discussions can continue for as long as it takes," her father continued.

"Then you would be free? You and Lily could marry?" she asked.

"Yes."

"That would be wonderful. Once we have Bryan back and your divorce is final, you and Lily can have a big wedding. The biggest the Double Crown has ever seen," Vanessa declared. "Victoria would have to come home for it."

"Let's not count our chickens too soon," her father suggested, but with a gentle smile for her.

After lunch, Dev said he had to see Wyatt Grayhawk and Sam Waterman. He hesitated and looked at her. She recognized the invitation to tag along and accepted at once.

Strapping herself into the SUV, she laughed almost happily. "We're making progress. Soon this will all be behind us. My family will be happy again. Then I'll work on you and your happiness," she vowed.

His smile was sardonic, but he would see, she promised her heart. Dev would admit they had a future...together.

The call came at six o'clock that evening. Gathered in the study were Ryan, Dev, Matthew, Claudia and Vanessa. Dev had asked that the rest of the family not be notified until the case was resolved. Two navy duffel bags sat on the floor near the door. Fifty million dollars in ransom money.

Claudia hugged the copy of the photo to her breast, a handkerchief clutched in her hand to catch the tears that slipped down her cheeks.

Vanessa patted her sister-in-law's hand and murmured for her to be brave, that Dev and Wyatt would soon have Bryan back. She willed it to be so.

"I'll deliver the money," Matthew said.

"I think they'll expect your father," Dev told him.

Ryan squeezed his son's shoulder. "We'll do whatever they say."

Matthew subsided with a curt nod.

The phone rang. Ryan picked it up. Dev was on his phone, connected to the men who were already tracing the call even as the phone rang.

"Ryan Fortune," her father said. "Yes, I'm ready." He picked up a pencil and paper. "Abandoned service station. An ice chest on the side. At eight?"

Vanessa clasped her hands to stop their trembling as her father listened, his jaw rigid with tension.

"Yes, I have it. Mixed bills, mostly hundreds, some fifties and twenties as stated in the note. Where will my grandson be? No! No money until I see the child."

Dev signaled him to agree.

"All right," Ryan said as if giving up. "I'll leave the money in the chest."

Dev shoved a note in front of him.

Ryan read it. "Provided I find instructions on where the baby is," he said to the kidnapper. "And provided the boy is close by. Wait a minute—" He turned to Dev. "He hung up. Did you get anything?"

Dev held up one finger, then gestured that her father should hang up. He punched a button and put his cell phone away. "Yeah, he was at a pay phone at the truck stop on the interstate. The highway patrol is on their way, but our man will be long gone with a five-minute start."

No one spoke when he narrowed his eyes in thought. Vanessa wondered what connection he was making.

At last he spoke. "We'll have plainclothes detectives all over the neighborhood around the gas station. He's sticking to the southwest side of the city. It's probably close to where he's holed up."

His cell phone rang. He listened, then said he would check the print, and hung up. He glanced at her father. "Would you rather I have someone else do the actual drop, sir?"

"No, I can handle it," Ryan assured him.

"All right. May I see the print of the baby?" he asked Claudia.

She surrendered it as if giving up the child.

"Charlie noticed the background of the picture. They propped the baby in a chair with pillows, but there's a window behind him. That's what caused the glare. There's an antenna in the background." He pointed to the print. "There. That's a radio station antenna. Charlie spotted it and called Wyatt. He's running a check on the maps of the county and all local stations for locations."

"Another mistake," Vanessa said. She stood, her spirits soaring. "He'll make another one and we'll get him. And his partners in crime."

Dev gave her a pointed glance. "The sheriff's men and the FBI will get them. You'll stay out of it."

"I'm going with you."

He shook his head. "You'll only be in the way. Are you ready, sir?" he asked her father.

Ryan picked up the duffel bags. "Let's go."

Vanessa said nothing as the two men who meant the most in her life walked out for their rendezvous with the kidnappers. Claudia went to the window.

"I hate them," she said. "Whoever did this. I hate them. I hope their souls rot in hell."

"They will," Matthew said grimly. "They will."

Vanessa looked at her watch. Not quite ten after six. Two hours to wait. If only she could help....

Twelve

Vanessa sat alone in the office after Dev and her father had left. Matthew and Claudia went to their quarters to wait. She hated doing nothing. Besides, she could be of help to Dev. After all, she knew what the cowboy who had worked at the ranch looked like. Dev and Wyatt and their deputies didn't, other than a composite drawing by a police artist.

On this thought, she dashed out and ran across the inner courtyard to the garage. Leaping into her sports car, she headed for town. Dev's SUV was in the parking lot across from the sheriff's office. She breathed a sigh of relief.

She parked beside him and waited.

Dev stopped when he saw her. His frown didn't bode well for her plan. He came over and rested his hands on her car while leaning down to the window. "What are you doing here?"

"Waiting for you. I want to go along."

"No."

"You haven't heard my plan," she accused. "You don't have a person on the case who has met James—or Jeremy, or whatever he's calling himself—face-to-face. I have. I can spot him for you when he picks up the money."

Dev gave her the closest thing to an impatient glare that she'd ever gotten from him.

"I think we'll be suspicious of anyone who stops and goes to the ice chest." He paused. "Go home, Beauty. You're a complication we don't need."

His tone was meant to be kind, but his words still rankled. Worse, he was right. What did she have to contribute to the arrest but another person for Dev to worry about? That was the real reason he was sending her away.

She nodded. "Okay. I can take a hint. My services aren't wanted." She touched his hand. "I couldn't bear it if you were hurt."

A ripple of emotion passed over his face. He took a breath and let it out slowly. "I'm wearing a bullet-proof vest."

She knew her words had touched him deeply in some way, but she didn't know how. There was no time to ask.

He stepped back. "I have to leave. Will you go back to the ranch and stay there?"

She nodded, worry eating at her. "Promise me you'll be careful. No unnecessary heroics and all that." She tried for a light tone and failed.

"I'll do my job."

"Come hell or high water," she added softly, leaning her head out the window. "Promise me, Dev. This one thing is all I'm asking of you."

The silence shifted and swirled between them. She needed this from him, she realized. This one acknowledgment from him of her feelings for him...and his for her. She waited, her eyes on his handsome, rugged face.

The moment stretched.

The tension crackled like static electricity, caught between their two bodies, between her needs and his denials, her love and his armor of distrust for that emotion.

"All right," she said at last. "It's okay. I shouldn't have…"

The words froze in her throat and she couldn't say them. She shook her head helplessly and fought the tears that wanted to fall and flood and wail out of her.

"I promise."

He spoke so softly she almost didn't hear him. The release of tension inside her was painful. A tear spilled down each cheek. She quickly brushed them away and hoped he didn't see. Dev was not one to give in to weakness. She shouldn't, either.

"Thank you." Settling behind the wheel, she started the engine and left the parking lot without a backward glance.

Dev pushed thoughts of Vanessa out of his head ruthlessly. He had a job to do. It was time to get on with it. The kidnappers might be watching at this moment and detect the undercover men moving into place.

He stopped at a fast-food restaurant and changed into black jeans in the men's room. A black shirt covered the bulletproof vest. He slipped his gun into its holster and pulled a denim jacket on to conceal the weapon. He checked his spare gun, which was strapped to his right leg. With black running shoes, he was ready for action.

After grabbing a burger, fries and soda, he headed

for the outskirts of town where the abandoned service station was located. It was an area of rundown warehouses, seedy hotels and seedier bars. He circled a block, then parked on the street, a few cars back and on the opposite corner from the station, and ate his meal.

At five before eight, Ryan Fortune drove his pickup onto the broken pavement and stopped beside the abandoned building. He glanced at two old cars parked at the back fence, looked around, then removed the bags of money from the cab of the truck. He carried them to the rusty ice chest and looked carefully inside. No notes or instructions that he could see.

A chill slid up his neck. He wondered if the kidnappers were watching him at this moment. Did they have his grandson? He surveyed the area. Not a soul in sight.

Picking up the bags, he headed for the truck. He wasn't leaving fifty million dollars without knowing where his grandson was and without knowing the boy was all right.

His cell phone rang as he turned. The sound jolted him like a bolt from a cattle prod.

"Yes?" he said, flipping it open. He heard only static noise, then the startled cry of a baby. "Bryan?" he said. "Is that my grandson?"

"Yes," a voice answered. "He'll be brought to the motel on the interstate at the Leather Bucket exit. A room will be registered in your name. Arrive alone and with the money thirty minutes from now. And don't call your FBI friend or the sheriff. We're watching you.''

Dev cursed. He'd heard every word from the mike he'd put in Ryan's vehicle. There were also transmitters in the bags and in the band around a stack of bills.

Wyatt's voice came over the frequency they were using on this operation. ''Freedom One, Freedom Two here.''

Dev picked up the unit. ''Go ahead.''

''I have a man on his way to the motel. Do you want the rest of us to move in?''

''Yes, but not close. Let's see if your man on the scene can get us a make on the vehicle the perps are using. Set up a relay to keep him in sight when he leaves. He might lead us to his lair and the other foxes. We'll take him there.''

''Ten-four.''

Dev put on a billed cap, pulling it low over his forehead. He headed south when he hit the interstate. At the Leather Bucket exit, he took the off-ramp and drove past the motel, a single-story building probably built in the fifties.

Only two cars there. He wished they'd had more business. It was easier to mingle in a crowd. Moving on, he noted the four country lanes leading off the road that became Main Street when it entered Leather Bucket a couple of miles farther west.

Turning around, he checked for a mile in the other direction. Two roads connected to the main one on that side. One of them went under the interstate and wound its way through the ranches east of the interstate. He checked a map of the area. There were radio towers out that way...the same ones in the photo with the Fortune grandson?

He got back on the interstate, drove to the next exit, crossed over and came back to the Leather Bucket ramp, exited and made another loop.

Wyatt came on the radio and advised that the undercover detective was checking into the motel at that moment. The cop was driving a black, crew-cab pickup. An older couple, driving a van, were the only other guests so far. No one had checked in under Ryan Fortune's name.

Dev had a sinking feeling. Something wasn't right.

Vanessa went to her father's study and plopped onto the plush recliner. After thirty seconds, she went to the desk and sat in the leather chair. Where Dev had sat.

She curled into the chair, her cheek against the high leather back. She inhaled deeply and thought she could detect Dev's clean, masculine scent on the chair.

Pressing closer, she felt a prick as her earring poked the tender spot behind her ear. She straightened and removed it. That's when she realized the left one was missing.

She looked around the chair, then the office. She went to her room and searched thoroughly. The earrings were a set of tiny pearls surrounded by emerald leaves. They had been a gift from her father for her sixteenth birthday. Sophia had been jealous until he had given her a whole set of emeralds for their wedding anniversary.

Not finding the missing one in her room or Dev's, Vanessa tried to think where else she had been. A scene came to mind. "Ah," she muttered.

She drove the half mile to the ranch office. There, she bent down beside the desk, as she had to retrieve the notepad for Cruz. And there it was, on the floor. She put it on again, making sure the fastener was secure.

The old-fashioned clock that Ruben kept on the windowsill filled the room with its busy ticking. Eight o'clock. Her father would be delivering the money now. She wanted to cross her fingers, spit over her shoulder three times and repeat all the other charms she'd believed in as a child.

She sat in the desk chair and idly straightened all the catalogs into two neat piles. She stacked the letters and memos in the In basket, then aligned the notepad evenly with the edge of the desk calendar. Picking up a pencil, she filled in the loops in the numbers.

Tiring of that, she pulled the notepad toward her. The light hit it at an angle. There were indentations in the paper where someone had written a message. Recalling the times she and Vicky had left secret messages for each other, she rubbed the pencil lightly over the embossed message. An address showed up. *RR1023. End. White, green shutters.*

The address rang a bell. She knew that place. Or thought she did. She and Victoria had gone to a white house with green shutters at the end of the ranch road many times.

An old woman had lived there. Their mom had bought brightly colored paper flowers from the woman for the ranch harvest fiesta for years. But the old woman had died long ago. No one lived in the house anymore.

The notepad wouldn't have lain behind the desk all this time. Rosita managed the office as well as the house when it came to cleanliness and order. She would have found it long ago. Besides, the paper was new, not old and turning brown at the edges. And who would have had cause to write down that address?

Cruz was looking for a ranch, but the handwriting wasn't his. A chill swept over her. Someone who needed a place to hide might find an abandoned homestead near the place he was working as a temporary cowboy very handy.

The memory of a flashing light came to her, of her and Victoria thinking it was neat because it winked at them. The light had been on an antenna. The antenna was located in the field behind the abandoned homestead! Like the one in the picture with the baby!

Leaping to her feet, she started from the office as if the hounds of hell were at her heels. She stopped. Dev! She had to call him to tell him she knew where the baby was! Grabbing up the phone, she punched in his cell phone number.

Dev hit the steering wheel with the flat of his hand as anger and frustration beat a tattoo of fury in his blood. They had been *that* close to nabbing the guy, but something had spooked him.

The cowboy had pulled into the motel parking lot on the heels of the detective, had studied the office where the cop was filling out a registration form while the owner processed his credit card, then had reversed and taken off. Ryan had arrived a minute later with the money.

The detective had alerted the team, and he and Dev had given chase. They had lost the guy on the back roads between Leather Bucket and San Antonio.

The detective pulled into a restaurant parking lot on the outskirts of San Antonio. Dev pulled up beside him.

"I've seen the cowboy before," the detective said. "I used to work as security in my off-duty hours at some of the local rodeos when I was on a regular beat. He must have recognized me and thought something was up."

Dev cursed. Of all the rotten luck. To have the one cop the perp might know as their point man. Hellfire!

He managed a wry smile for the young, worried officer. "Win some, lose some. We might as well go home and wait to see what they do next."

"I could stick around—"

"Nah. They won't be back. We'll just have to wait to see what they do."

They talked to Wyatt, then signed off. Dev said good-night and left. A picture of a baby propped in a chair kept popping into his mind. He stopped and studied the map.

Shaking his head at his probable foolishness, he headed southeast of town. He might just drive out a couple of country roads, maybe cruise by those towers—

The ring of the cell phone interrupted his thoughts. He answered with an annoyed, "Yeah?"

"Dev, I know where the baby is! I know where the

farmhouse is! And the antenna with the winking light!''

He recognized the excited voice in a heartbeat. Her words didn't make sense. "Slow down. Start at the beginning and tell me what you're shouting about.''

"The baby. Bryan,'' she said impatiently. "I know where he is. At the end of an old ranch road— RR1023. That's where Vicky and I used to go with Mom when we were kids. We liked the winking light. And that's on the antenna in the picture of Bryan!''

The hair stood up on his neck. "How do you know this is the place?''

She told him about finding a notepad in the ranch office and about seeing the indentation of writing, then rubbing over it with a pencil. "The baby's there. I know he is. We can go get him while the kidnappers are picking up the money,'' she finished triumphantly.

He frowned heavily. "*I'll* go get him. You stay put, you hear? The kidnappers could return at any moment.'' He didn't go into detail on why this could be true.

"The baby will be frightened. He'll need someone from the family with him. I'm his aunt—''

"No! You'll damn well stay there, or else.'' He calmed down with an effort. "Look, I appreciate the information, but it probably doesn't mean a thing.''

He sensed her disappointment.

"I'll check it out,'' he said. "You're less than ten minutes from the place. If the baby's there, I'll call you to come get him. Okay?''

But not until after he and Wyatt got the kidnappers.

"Okay,'' she agreed reluctantly. "Promise you'll call?''

"Promise." He hung up. He'd never met a woman who set such store by promises. He would call, but only after the case was wrapped up nice and tidy. But first, he would check it out. No use sending the whole county sheriff's department on a false run if this didn't pan out.

Vanessa paced the office. Frustration and worry ate at her. She hated waiting while events unfolded close by. The baby would be terrified when another stranger grabbed him and took off. Frowning, she considered, then shook her head as if arguing with an unseen opponent. But, darn it, she knew she could be of help. Bryan would need her.

Making up her mind, she jammed her old gray felt Stetson over her hair. After a second's deliberation, she opened the safe and removed a .38 semiautomatic from its box. She inserted the bullet clip.

After tucking the weapon into her waistband, she wrote a note for Ruben and Cruz, telling them where she was going and why. If anything happened, they would know what to do.

However, she really didn't expect any trouble. She and Dev would slip in, grab the baby and get away while the men were gone. Besides, Wyatt would have arrested them by now.

They might have left someone behind to watch Bryan, though. Hence the gun. On a ranch, a person learned to be prepared for unforeseen emergencies.

She drove down the country road at high speed, taking the curves at a fast clip, her low-slung sports car hugging the road. That the kidnappers might be only a few miles from the ranch added insult to injury, as if they thumbed their noses at her family.

Then again, like Dev said, this might be a wild-goose chase and the cowboy who'd been at the ranch might be nowhere near.

As she neared the old house, she slowed to a crawl. Finding an overgrown trail, she turned onto it and pulled up under a leafy tree next to the fence that circled the property. She climbed out of the car.

Clouds covered the last rays of sunset on the horizon, and twilight cast a gloom over the landscape. Her tan and green clothing were close to camouflage colors. She tucked her hair into her hat.

Dev was probably inside, but she decided caution was the better part of valor. She crept as quietly as possible through the field toward the house where all was dark, except for one sliver of light shining from the back.

Her heart raced, and she paused, hidden behind an old lean-to that had once sheltered a winter's supply of wood. No vehicles of any sort around. Where was Dev?

The silence drummed in her ears. She realized it was her heartbeat. She checked the gun, made sure the clip was secure, then hid it in the small of her back so her blouse would cover the bulge.

Taking a deep breath, she sped across the weed-choked yard. At the house, in a slit in the curtains, she peered into the dim room. Her heart jumped to her throat.

Driving as fast as he could, Dev cruised the road that had once been paved but had fallen into disrepair.

The pavement looked like an alligator hide. Felt like one, too. He winced as his tire dropped into a pothole with a lurch that shook the entire frame of the vehicle.

Coming around a curve, he spotted the tower off to his right. It was well back from the road. He kept an eye out for a road to the right that would take him to it…or to a house where a baby was being kept hostage.

He spotted an overgrown road that was mostly two ruts through grass and weeds. When he pulled in, he threw on the brakes. His heart stopped as suddenly as the SUV, then thudded painfully.

A smart sports car nestled, nearly hidden, under the branches of some scrub oak growing along an old fence row. Three guesses who it belonged to, and the first two didn't count. The darkness roiled and churned in him. He could sense danger with that sixth sense cops developed.

He pulled up under the leafy overhang, checked his gun, added several clips to his jacket pocket and headed across the field which lay in dark gray shadows between him and the house in the distance.

Beyond the house, a radio tower winked its light at him, off and on, off and on. At that moment he heard a shot. He broke into a run, fear eating his heart alive.

No one appeared to be in the house.

Vanessa worked her way all around it, peering into every window. Going to the back door, she tried the knob. It wasn't locked. She eased inside.

Her knees went weak at a loud creak from a floorboard. She stopped dead-still and waited. Nothing.

She tiptoed across the kitchen and into the hall. She paused again. The silence mocked her fears. She slipped into the back bedroom, which was empty except for one thing.

A baby lay on a blanket, overturned kitchen chairs forming a pen around him. He was asleep.

Hands trembling, she bent over a chair and carefully lifted Bryan into her arms. He roused and wrinkled his little forehead in a frown. She swayed from side to side, rocking him back to sleep. He nodded off again.

She turned toward the door. Her heart hardly dared beat, she wanted so desperately to be silent, to get out of there and get home.

A noise toward the back alerted her. She heard the kitchen door open and close, then footsteps inside. From outside, she heard the sound of a truck engine and the crunch of its tires on gravel. It came to a sliding halt.

Dev, she thought in relief.

Someone slammed the front door. Running footsteps toward the kitchen. "What's up?" she heard a man ask.

The person she'd heard come into the house first, she thought. He must have been outside while she'd been sneaking around the house. Her heart sank. Where was Dev?

The other man cursed viciously. "It was a setup," he said. "There was a cop at the motel, pretending to check in, when I drove up. I recognized him. He used to work the rodeos around here in his spare time. Son of a—"

His words faded as he stomped into the kitchen.

Vanessa strained to hear, but the words were muffled. Her heart sank when she heard them both come up the hallway.

She clutched the baby to her with her left hand and used her right to slip the gun from its hiding place. She wasn't going to give up her nephew if she had to shoot both of them. But she hoped it wouldn't come to that.

The bedroom door flew open and hit the wall.

"That's far enough, gentlemen," she said. Her voice was cool, her hand steady. "The party's over."

"A woman," one of the men said in surprise.

"The Fortune brat," the other snarled.

She recognized him as the cowboy who had worked on the ranch a few months that spring and summer. His eyes blazed with fury. She was in a tight spot.

How was she going to tie up two men with a baby in one hand and a gun in the other?

"Face the wall, hands on the wall above your heads," she ordered, motioning with the gun.

The cowboy started to turn, then threw his car keys at her face. She flinched, but she also squeezed the trigger.

A red stain blossomed on the cowboy's arm. It didn't stop him, though. While his partner hung back, he lunged forward and knocked the gun upward. The second bullet went through the ceiling.

She fell to the floor, the baby still clutched to her side. Vaguely, she heard the child's cries of terror. The cowboy fell half on top of her. She thrust him aside and brought the gun around once more. But his hand was on her wrist, forcing the muzzle toward the wall. Then he hit her with his fist.

Light exploded in her eyes, washed over her, then blinked out. She fell into total darkness, holding on to the gun and the baby for dear life. She would die before she let him take either from her.

"Hold it," a commanding voice said from the doorway.

She struggled back from the abyss. Her sight cleared. Dev stood in the room, a gun in his hand. To her horror, the cowboy grabbed her hand. She felt the hard press of a finger over hers on the gun's trigger and heard the explosion.

"Oh, no, please no," she pleaded. In the pause that followed, she brought her right hand up with all her might and hit the kidnapper in the face.

He nearly broke her fingers, but she held the gun fast.

"Back off. Into the corner," Dev said.

She lost her hat, and her hair cascaded over her face. She pushed it aside, her eyes wide. "Dev," she whispered and tried to rise, to go to him. "Shh, shh," she murmured to the crying baby.

She couldn't see any blood. He'd told her he was wearing a vest. Relief poured through her.

It was short-lived. The partner appeared in the doorway behind Dev. He pointed a shotgun at her. "Drop it, or the girl gets it."

Dev neatly stepped aside and pivoted. He pointed his gun at the newcomer. "Standoff," he said, his smile mocking.

It seemed a lifetime, but it couldn't have been more than a second before the cowboy, standing and holding his arm, spoke up. "Shoot, man. You can get them both in one shot." He picked up the set of keys.

The other man considered. "Nobody said nuthin' about killing when I came in on this deal. I ain't shootin' no cop, or no woman and baby, either."

The cowboy cursed. He looked at her, then Dev. He grinned suddenly, a macabre snarl of his lips. "He won't shoot. He's afraid the woman and kid will get killed. Then Fortune will strip his hide and lay him out for the buzzards to fight over. Let's get out of here." Blood ran between his fingers. Sweat stood out on his forehead.

"Yeah," his partner agreed. He pointed the shotgun at Dev. "Stay put. I don't want to have to kill you and the woman, but I will. Understand?"

Dev nodded. He kept his gun on the man.

"Just don't move for five minutes. We'll be gone by then. I'll shoot you on sight if you come out."

The two men backed out and closed the door.

She looked at Dev. "Shouldn't we—"

"No." He sat on the floor, his back propped against the wall. "We wait." He gestured toward Bryan with the gun. "See if you can quiet him."

She remembered seeing a pacifier on the blanket. She retrieved it and, crooning to her nephew, held him against her and rocked back and forth from the waist until his sobs died away. He stared at her with big solemn eyes and sucked hard on the fake nipple.

From outside they heard the kidnappers' vehicle start up, then take off down the gravel drive. In less than a moment, the sound faded. Silence enclosed them.

"We can leave," she said. A smile broke over her face. "We have the baby. We're safe. We can leave."

His smile was sardonic. "You go on, Beauty. Take the baby to the ranch. Don't stop for anyone or any thing. I'll put in a call for Wyatt."

She noticed then that his left hand was pressed against his chest. Pain riddled his eyes.

"You're hurt," she said, puzzled. "Were you hit?"

"I think your bullet smashed a rib," he said, a laconic smile on his face. "It's nothing." He paused and grimaced with pain. "Call Wyatt...my cell phone."

She stared in shocked horror as he slumped to the floor. After laying the baby in his makeshift pen, she knelt beside Dev. She examined him with her eyes and gently with her hands. She saw no blood and felt no broken bones.

As carefully as she could, she straightened him. His breath caught in a gasp, stopped, then resumed in a raspy groan. She opened the black shirt. Finding the tabs, she opened the bulletproof vest. There was no blood on the white T-shirt, either.

Carefully, she eased it from his jeans. Then she saw the bruise...fist-size, furiously red, already turning a sickening purple.

Hands shaking, she searched his jacket pockets and found the phone. She turned it on, waited for it to find its signal, then called Wyatt.

"Wyatt, I need help," she said as soon as he answered. "Dev is...he's been shot. His vest saved him, but he could have internal injuries."

"Tell me where you are," Wyatt broke in.

"Road 1023, the old house at the end on the right, east of the Leather Bucket exit on the interstate."

"Roger that. Do you need an ambulance?"

"Yes. He's…he's passed out."

"All right. Stay calm. Is anyone with you?"

"The baby. Just me and the baby. The kidnappers left. In a black truck."

"We'll be there in fifteen minutes."

"Hurry," she said, her voice trembling. "Hurry."

She turned the phone off. She brushed the hair off Dev's forehead. He was so still. Her heart clenched in fear. He couldn't die. He couldn't.

"I forbid it," she whispered to him. "You have to stay. For us. For our children. For the future. It can't happen without you. You're the one I need to make my dreams come true. Oh, love, love, don't die…"

His breathing was shallow, raspy. Each breath was taken with obvious pain. Each time he stopped, her heart withered. Each time he resumed with a painful gasp, she gasped, too. She was sure his ribs were broken. Nothing could stop the guilty knowledge that she had put him in danger, that it was her gun, with her holding it, that had fired the bullet.

If he died, she knew who to blame. The fault would be hers, hers alone. Her and her impatient, know-it-all ways.

If he died…if he died…

The words echoed over and over inside her. Tears ached behind her eyes. She wouldn't let them fall. She didn't deserve the easy release of tears.

It was an eon before she heard the sirens on the country road.

Thirteen

Vanessa paced the waiting room, the baby sleeping against her chest. Dev was in emergency surgery. Wyatt and his men had set up roadblocks around the county. Her father and Matthew and Claudia were on their way to town.

Hearing their voices at the elevator, she went to the door. "In here," she called softly.

Claudia gave a sob and rushed forward, nearly falling in her eagerness to get to her son. Matthew caught her arm and steadied his wife. They crossed the hall, her father on their heels.

"Oh, my God," Claudia whispered. She held out her arms.

Vanessa laid the sleeping child against his mother's breast. Joy, too painful to be shared without tears, filled her eyes. Matthew crowded close to his wife and son.

Claudia's tears fell on the blanket as she rocked back and forth with her child at last in her arms again.

Ryan put his arm across Vanessa's shoulders and handed Claudia his handkerchief. He grabbed tissues from a box on the table for himself, Matthew and Vanessa.

"Sit, darling," Matthew urged.

They took seats on the sofa, Vanessa and Ryan on

the nearby chairs. Claudia tenderly tucked little Bryan into the crook of her arm and pulled the light blanket open so she could examine her baby herself. She gasped as if in horror, then started shaking her head.

"No, no," she moaned. "This isn't my baby. This isn't Bryan."

"Baby's grow so fast at this age," Vanessa said in a soothing voice. "He's gained some weight and his face is rounder—"

Claudia thrust the baby toward Matthew, still shaking her head. "I'd know my own child. This isn't Bryan. It isn't!" Her voice rose hysterically.

Matthew took the baby, studied him, then Vanessa, his expression uncertain, questioning.

"It has to be. This was the baby I found at the house. The kidnappers were there. This is Bryan." She nodded reassuringly at Claudia. "The pediatrician here at the hospital examined him. He has the double crown birthmark. I saw it myself. He just looks different because he's older—"

"No!" Claudia screamed at her. "This is not my child!" She bent over and buried her face in her hands. "Oh, God, my baby…my baby…oh, dear God."

Matthew caught her shoulder as she slumped toward the floor. Ryan leaped to his feet. He helped Matthew lay her on the sofa. Vanessa tucked a pillow under her head.

Ryan and Matthew stared at the baby, who opened his eyes at that moment and studied the two men bending over him. He hesitated, then a big smile widened his mouth. A string of drool rolled over his chubby chin.

"She's right," Matthew said. "I don't know who this is, but it isn't…it can't be Bryan. He favors our baby, this one…but he's heavier…bigger."

"Whose could he be?" Vanessa asked. "This is crazy. It has to be Bryan. He has the birthmark."

"We can do a footprint. Here at the hospital," Matthew said. "I'll call the pediatrician. He's a friend."

Vanessa reclaimed the baby while Matthew went to call the baby doctor. Her heart stopped when a surgeon came to the room.

"Kincaid family?" he said.

"Here." She cleared her throat. "We're here for him. I'm his fiancée."

"He's doing fine. He'll be in recovery for an hour before being moved to a room."

"How bad was he hurt?" her father asked.

"The vest stopped the bullet, but the rib was smashed from the force. A couple of splinters stuck in his heart." At her gasp, the doctor smiled. "He's too stubborn to let a little thing like that stop him. He'll be okay."

"How long will he be in the hospital?" she asked.

"A week. Less if he doesn't develop a fever."

She nodded in relief.

The surgeon lifted a hand to her lip. "You need a couple of stitches here. Come on down to the station and I'll take care of it."

Startled, she handed the alert baby to her father and went with the surgeon. He cleaned her lower lip, numbed it and put two neat stitches in the split caused by the cowboy's fist and her teeth.

"Your FBI friend told me to take care of you,"

the surgeon said while he worked. "He wanted me to do it before I checked him out."

"He's like that," she mumbled, then flinched.

"Don't smile very much for a couple of days," the doctor advised with a grin. "Hold this in place until it quits bleeding again."

"When can I see Dev?" She held the gauze swab against her numb lip.

"The nurse will tell you when he's taken to a room."

"Thanks." She returned to the waiting room.

Her father glanced up from the sofa where he played with the baby, who was smiling and cooing. "This is a heck of a mess. Claudia came around. Matthew ordered a sedative and had her put to bed here. He's going to spend the night, too. The pediatrician who checked the baby is going to compare his footprint with the one on file tomorrow."

"You think this isn't Bryan?"

Her father shook his head. "I don't know. He sort of looks like him, but not exactly. I assumed my memory was at fault, that, like you said, he's grown. But...I don't know. He isn't the same. This may not be Bryan."

"But the birthmark—"

"I know. We looked at it—Matthew and the doctor and I. This is my grandson, but he may not be Matthew and Claudia's child."

"My God," she whispered. "Whose child is he?"

Ryan's face hardened. "I'm going to request my sons and nephews be at the ranch tomorrow to discuss that very thing after the footprint is verified. No Fortune ever turned his back on his own flesh."

* * *

Vanessa felt a touch on her arm. She jerked upright off the sheet. Pain ripped through her head. Her bottom lip felt twice its usual size, and her tongue seemed to be made of some soft, gluey substance.

The silence closed around her. The hospital was eerily quiet at four in the morning. Dev hadn't woken yet from his surgery. It worried her, this stillness from a man she'd always known as controlled but forceful and dynamic.

His arm jerked again. She noted his eyes moving under his lids. He was probably dreaming of them and their close call. She didn't know if she could forgive herself for holding the gun that shot him, even though she hadn't actually pulled the trigger.

The terror of that moment would live in her forever. And the guilt. In spite of the doctor's assurances, she still wasn't convinced Dev would be all right. She imagined splinters sticking in his heart. Such a brave, true heart.

She rose and bent over him. "Don't you die," she whispered. "Don't you dare die."

Her heart nearly stopped when he opened his eyes a slit and stared at her. A smile broke through her worry.

"No more promises," he said hoarsely.

She shook her head, giddy with relief. "Not good enough. Give me your word or I'll hound you to eternity."

He gave a snort that ended in a gasp. "You'll already do that. Not something...I can stop."

"How do you feel, really?" She gave him an encouraging smile, her love soft and caring and euphoric within her.

Dev didn't smile back. He blinked his eyes wearily. "Okay. You…go home."

"No way. As if I'd leave you."

"Knew you'd be stubborn. But…don't want you…here. Go home." His voice faded to a whisper of effort on the last words.

She tilted her head slightly, unsure what he was saying. She glanced at the window. "It's nearly dawn. I've slept all night. I feel fine."

He grimaced impatiently. His fingers dug into her arm. "Listen," he ordered tersely. "Go…home."

The nurse bustled in. "I thought you must be awake. The monitor is beeping like crazy. Lie still. You two can't dance until the fat lady sings. That won't be for another week at the earliest."

She laughed cheerily at her own humor, adjusted the IV drip speed and stuck an electronic thermometer in his ear. She took his pulse, then released his wrist with a frown.

"Is something bothering you? Are you hurting?"

"No." He bobbed his chin toward Vanessa. "Tell her to get out of here."

The nurse glanced from him to her and back again. "You want your fiancée to leave?"

"She's not—" He gestured with a hand, then clenched his teeth at the agony this produced. "She's not my fiancée."

"You are in pain." The nurse turned a scolding gaze on Vanessa. "Perhaps you'd better leave. He seems agitated."

Vanessa stood, uncertain what to do. A knot formed in her chest and rose to her throat.

Leaning over her stubborn lover, she murmured,

"I'll be back. You won't get rid of me so easily as that, Devin Kincaid. I always get what I want, and I want you. Put that in your pipe and smoke it," she ordered softly.

"You're trouble," he said doggedly, sounding weary beyond belief. "Thought I could keep you separate from the investigation...but you interfered."

She stood there, dead-still, her heart tripping over itself in apology. "I know. I shouldn't have gone...I didn't mean to interfere. It was just...I thought I could help," she finished miserably.

"Nearly got us both killed," he reminded her grimly. He shook his head slightly and grimaced with pain. "I heard that shot...and forgot twenty years of training. Didn't call for backup...just ran like hell...because of...because of you."

He was breathing hard by the time he got the words out. His eyes bored two holes right through her heart. The nurse stood on the other side of the bed, her eyes wide as she took in the strange confrontation.

Vanessa blanched. "I'm so sorry," she whispered around the pain that filled her chest.

He didn't acknowledge her words. "When I saw the house...I was pretty sure we had them. The tower was in the field, like you said...should have called Wyatt then...would have trapped the men and found out their partners."

She had flogged herself all the long hours of the night, wishing she'd done differently, but his words made her realize how badly she had messed up. Because of her, the kidnappers had gotten away, he had been injured...

"Stupid little rich girl. Always has to have her way. Stupid me…for letting her…"

She wrapped her hands around the metal railing as dizziness washed over her. She held on and listened to the terrible truth he spoke.

"I know," she said when he fell silent. "Dev, *I know*. If I could turn back the clock, I would."

She faced his unrelenting gaze as steadily as she could, hating herself for having caused harm to him.

He closed his eyes. "Go home, Beauty…the fairy tale has ended…happily for the baby and his parents. For me…for us…this case is closed. For good."

She stood there as if carved from stone for the longest time. Outside, birds chirped. The sun shone. Cars sped down the street. The world carried on. The shattering of a heart didn't even cause a hitch in its busy schedule.

Without another word, she picked up her battered Stetson and walked out into the shimmering dawn of another hot day.

Dev lay there listening to her footsteps long after they were gone. He glanced at the nurse, who busied herself checking his bandages. She looked rather stunned and maybe a little stricken by the incident she had witnessed.

The way he felt.

The way those green, green eyes had looked while he said the words guaranteed to send her away. He had hammered in every nail, doing it and knowing he was doing it, knowing he was hurting her, knowing he was delivering rabbit punches straight to the heart.

The most vulnerable spot in the human body. It had been necessary.

Best. This way was best. For a while he'd lived in a fool's dream, thinking maybe she was right, that there could be a future for them.

Stupid. Really stupid. He had never had that kind of future, the one with the family and the living happily ever after, at all. Hadn't he learned that simple fact long ago, as a boy and again as a man, standing beside a coffin in the hot Texas sun?

For a short time he had let himself forget, had even let himself consider a future. It had been foolish to take that kind of chance. This time, he was the one who had paid for his foolish dreams, but if he let her stay, she could be the one hurt next time. He wouldn't take that chance. Not with her. She was all the good things of life—the laughter, the warmth, the sweet raging desire, the peace afterward, the joy of living. She was all those and more. She was the one thing he would never regret and never forget.

"She'll find someone," he explained to the silent nurse. "The glow will return. It's just dimmed a little now. It'll come back."

Memories rushed at him. He saw Vanessa's eyes shining with tears as they made love, heard her sexy little cries of pleasure...saw them riding through green meadows, saw other things as memories changed to fantasy.

Vanessa, holding a child in her arms, tucked right up next to her heart. The child was hers. His and hers. For a while he'd even thought it might be possible. Fool.

For twenty years he'd lived alone, without longing

for those things that would never be. She'd opened
the door where hopes had lain fallow within him with
the force of just a smile. She'd opened the door and
let the sunlight fill the darkness. For a brief moment
she'd even turned him into a believer.

But he should have known better. He had known.

When that first shot had rung out, he'd faced the
blackest moment in his life. He had thought she might
be dead. God in Heaven, it wasn't a thought he could
live with. Not then. Not now. Not ever.

He'd learned his lesson. Never would he tempt fate
again. The darkness roiled in him, triumphant once
more.

Slowly, slowly, he forced the rusty door back on
its hinges until finally it closed with a forlorn sound
that echoed in his soul. Hope was back in its place,
locked into the black hole of despair where, he'd
learned long ago, it belonged.

And she, the loveliest of all lovely dreams, would
find her true love, a younger man, one who could
make her wishes come true, as he could not. She
would be happy. It was the one thing he made himself
believe.

Dev thanked the nurse for the ride without being
sardonic about it, then lifted himself out of the wheel-
chair and walked to his SUV, newly repaired from its
brush with the tree, its paint fresh, its tires new. After
eight days in the hospital, he should have felt re-
newed. He didn't.

Wyatt, who'd had a deputy drive the vehicle to the
hospital, smiled and waved, then drove off after his

man climbed into the passenger side of the sheriff's truck.

The interior of the SUV was blessedly cool. Dev winced as he reached for the seat belt, but managed to get it fastened. He put the truck in gear and drove himself home.

The house was pleasant and shining when he let himself in the front door. Delicious smells enticed him to the kitchen. There he found what he had half expected, half hoped for and totally feared.

Vanessa.

She'd come to visit him every day at the hospital, despite his refusal to see her. He'd tried the only way he knew how to push her away—for her sake. But she was stubborn in her naive faith. He closed his eyes and let the anger simmer and bubble and boil. It was time she learned a Fortune didn't always get her own way.

"Hi. Lunch in ten minutes. Take a seat. You like raspberry iced tea? It's on the table. I have plain, if you would prefer it."

"This is fine." He went to the table, which was covered with a green plaid tablecloth and set with Mexican patterned dishes he'd never seen before. He sat so he could watch her while she worked, her hands skillful at the chore of cooking, a fact that never failed to astonish him.

As if a Fortune would ever have to lift her hand to a skillet if she didn't want to.

She set a platter of shrimp and vegetables between their plates. A colorful bowl held hot, buttered rolls.

"Salad," she murmured, and went to the refrigerator.

The meal was superb, as he'd known it would be. She did nothing by halves. He ate until he was filled, because the food was good, because it was cooked by her, because he wanted to postpone as long as possible what he was going to say.

"I suppose Wyatt told you the real news about the baby?" she asked.

"That it's a Fortune baby but not the missing one? Yes, he told me. Your family must be in a quandary."

"That's putting it mildly. Wyatt said we should keep that news a secret for now. Until he can find out what's going on." She paused and gazed at him, her eyes warm and loving. "Matthew and Claudia are keeping Taylor—that's what they're calling the new baby—until we find out who its parents are. We're still left with Bryan missing."

"It's been a strange case."

"I understand the FBI considers their part done. My father said you wouldn't be back."

"That's right. The case isn't closed, but without those two men or more information, we're stymied."

"I know. Do you know where you'll be assigned after you return to work?"

"No."

She nodded and fell silent after that.

He didn't tell her he was thinking of retiring from the FBI. With his service time counted, he had his twenty years in. Sam Waterman was urging him to come work for him in his detective agency. That would mean staying in San Antonio permanently. He wasn't sure he was up to that. But he would think about it later. When he had all the time in the world.

"Thanks for the meal," he said, finishing before she did, his tone deliberately offhand, almost flippant.

She shot him a considering glance, then picked up the used plates. She replaced them with two perfectly baked flans flanked by slices of berries.

He grimly ate the dessert. He pushed it away, then caught her wrist before she could rise again. "I don't want to see you again," he said flatly.

"Why?"

"That Fortune confidence," he murmured. "Most women would have given up long before this."

"I'm not most women."

He had never thought that. She was fire and water, earth and air. She was like no one he'd ever before encountered. For a moment he envisioned her in his arms, her eyes sparkling like grass laved with dew, her face aglow, her beautiful fiery hair spread across the pillow they shared. That image belonged behind the door, too. He forced it away.

"This isn't going to work, Beauty. No way. No how. Let's just end it gracefully."

She propped her elbows on the table and leaned her chin on her hands. He could sense a quietness in her that he'd never encountered before, a careful waiting that wasn't part of her nature, a wariness that was new.

A fist took hold of his heart. She was hurting, and there wasn't a thing he could do about it.

"Why?" she asked. "Why not just ride it out and see where it goes and how long it lasts? Would that be so terrible?"

Ruthless. He had to be ruthless. Because none of what she suggested could ever be. "Yes."

"Liar."

She spoke softly, teasing him, but her eyes...the hurt was there. Better a little now than a lot later on. She swallowed, but said nothing more.

He looked her in the eye. "You nearly got yourself killed last week. If you're going to act stupid, I'd rather you didn't kill me in the bargain."

Guilt skipped across her face.

"If you hadn't interfered, I would have called for backup and we would have nabbed those men. As it was, we barely got out of there alive."

"That was foolish of me. I promise never to do anything so foolish again," she said, her face earnest.

"You just don't get it. I'm not willing to take that chance on what is, after all, a casual affair. A fling isn't worth either of our lives. My work is dangerous. I don't have time to worry about an amateur butting in and messing things up."

Her eyes went wide. He watched the shock of his words ripple through her body. She blinked. Then her chin came up. The Fortune pride. He was counting on it to save him, to save them both.

Leaning toward him, she met his gaze without flinching. "Is that what it was between us, Dev? A fling? That's all?"

"That's all."

He saw her chest move as she took a careful breath. "Okay," she said. She got up and proceeded to silently clean up the kitchen. When it was neat, she picked up a tiny purse with a long, thin strap.

"You're throwing away something good, but I can't force you to accept the gift of our love. I know that you've been hurt. I think, given time, we could get past that. But you have to trust, Dev. I can't do it for you.''

She put the strap over her shoulder and walked out of his house. Out of his life.

It was better this way. He'd seen the hope slowly beaten out of his mother. His own had died when he'd watched them lower his dad into the ground and known life was never going to be what he'd hoped. He'd seen Stan's wife stand beside her husband's grave with her children at her side, her eyes beyond hope.

Outside, a car started, then left. There had never been a chance in hell for them anyway. He listened to the silence for a time before giving in to physical pain. He took two pills the doc had prescribed and went to bed.

Fourteen

Dev parked his truck in the shade and sat there staring at the hacienda baking in the afternoon sun. September was proving to be as hot as August.

Ryan Fortune had called and asked him to join him for a wrap-up meeting on the kidnapping. Dev wasn't sure about being there. He was officially off the case. Off everything, in fact, he admitted fatalistically.

He was dressed in jeans and a white shirt. He wore black sneakers. Theoretically, he was still in recuperation and had the whole month off before the doctor would okay his return to work. Sitting in the house all day was driving him up the wall. He had seized upon the excuse to get out.

He laughed silently, mockingly, at himself. Now that he was here, he was afraid to get out of the truck. He had no doubt that his redheaded, green-eyed nemesis would be at the meeting. He would live through it.

He sighed and forced himself out of the truck and to the front door. Rosita opened it at once.

"Come in," she invited, her face wreathed in smiles. "It is good to see you again."

He returned her smile and stepped into the cool interior. "Thanks for the food you've sent. It's been a lifesaver. My cooking is registered with the FBI as a lethal weapon."

She closed the door and gave him a scolding glance. "You know who sent the food. And cooked most of it."

A flush crept up his neck.

She nodded her head regally. "Señor Ryan is in his study. You are to join him."

Dev walked down the short hallway. The door was open. His heart beat hard, almost painfully. He went in. There was no one there but the Fortune patriarch.

"Good afternoon," Dev said, stepping forward and holding out his hand. The darkness stirred relentlessly.

Ryan came around the desk and shook his hand, clasping his shoulder warmly at the same time. "Well, you're looking better than the last time I saw you."

Dev, Wyatt, Sam and Ryan had held a couple of meetings in his hospital room. The head nurse hadn't liked that. She said his temperature went up each time.

"I'm feeling much better, sir."

"Have a seat. Rosita brought us some tea."

He handed Dev a frosty glass of raspberry tea. Dev recalled his first visit to this house and his awkwardness with the elder Fortune and his determined daughter. This time he removed the mint leaf and orange slice, laid them on the side of the coaster and took a refreshing drink.

"Did Wyatt tell you about the infant seat?"

"No, sir." Dev looked a question at his host.

"It was in the nursery the day of the kidnapping.

It was checked for fingerprints, but no one thought to ask about it. The maid brought it out of the closet yesterday and asked Claudia if she wanted to use it again. Claudia said it wasn't Bryan's carrier. She hadn't brought his in from the car when they arrived for the christening. She'd carried him in her arms and laid him in the crib.''

The hair stood up on Dev's neck as it always did when he found an important piece of evidence. ''Who does it belong to?''

Ryan shook his head. ''That's the mystery. No one here knows. I thought you might work on solving this puzzle while you're recovering. If you feel up to it. You can direct Sam and his man, McCoy, in the investigation. Of course, you would need to stay out here.''

Dev stared at the carpet. Something sweet and fragile and hopeless struggled within him to be heard. The darkness beat it back. ''Sir—''

''I asked you to let her down easy,'' Ryan broke in, his gaze sternly reproving. ''You have a lot to make up for with my daughter.''

''Sir...'' Dev took another long drink, buying time while he tried to think. The struggle resumed, stronger this time, more insistent. Hope beat at the rusty door.

''I know she's impulsive and headstrong. But she's also loyal and honest, and arrow straight. She'd make a fine wife, if I do say so.''

Dev's heart pounded so hard, his chest was one big ache. He breathed deeply until he'd calmed a bit. ''I hadn't considered marriage. My work...my partner died. He left a wife and two kids behind.''

''My first wife died of cancer.'' Ryan fixed a laser

beam on him from eyes that were discerning and candid. "Life doesn't come with guarantees, man. My girl is no wilting violet. She's a Texas bluebonnet. She's tough and resilient."

"Yes, sir," Dev agreed, reaching for a light tone. This was a joke fate was playing on him. Her father wasn't really telling him to marry her, that he shouldn't let the fact that she could have been killed stop him. "You left off stubborn, willful and opinionated."

Ryan stopped his tirade. A grin split his face. "I assumed you were already acquainted with those traits. Well? You going to handle the investigation?"

Dev tried to think, to put reason ahead of need and the stark hunger that urged him to find her and claim her for his own. The rusty door trembled and creaked like a house in a violent storm.

He thought of life and how it had been before he met her, of how the darkness never left him now. He stared at the window and the slant of the afternoon sun across the courtyard. He could feel its heat through the window.

Light.

He knew what it was to live without it. How would it be to bask in its warmth every day? "I think I have no choice," he said slowly, blinking as if just coming out of a dark theater into the sun.

The father lifted his glass and waited. Dev picked his up. They made a silent toast, then drank.

"She's down at the stables," Ryan said upon taking his seat again.

Dev gulped the spicy tea. He nodded. "If that's all?"

Ryan nodded, walked him to the front door and saw him off. Dev drove down and parked in front of the ranch office. No redheaded female was in any of the paddocks. He went to the office and opened the door.

Cruz was inside.

"Where's Vanessa?" he asked, seeing no need to exchange pleasantries.

"Who wants to know?" the horse trainer replied.

Dev paused a beat. "Her fiancé."

One eyebrow shot up. "She took a ride. I'd guess she was up at the ridge."

Dev pressed a hand to the scar on his chest and tested its soreness. "Can you saddle up the roan for me?"

A slow smile spread over the other man's face. "That I can do." He went outside. In a few minutes he brought the big horse around front. Bending, he cupped his hands and looked at Dev expectantly.

Dev grinned. "I'm no English lady, but I'll take you up on the offer." He put his foot into Cruz's hands and let the cowboy heft him onto the tall mount. "Thanks."

"No problem. I put some jerky and stuff in the saddlebag. In case you miss supper."

Dev nodded his thanks and took off. He let the gelding go at a fast walk. He couldn't handle anything bouncier than that, he discovered. The trip took an hour.

He left the roan in the little glen with the horse she'd ridden. He found her where he thought she'd be, sitting near the mouth of the cave, her back against a rock. Her hat lay on the ground beside her. Her eyes were closed.

"I knew I'd find you here," he said.

Her eyes flew open, startled at first, then hooded. But not before he saw the wounded depths of her.

"Your grieving place."

"I'm not…"

She let the denial dangle in midair between them as she leaned against the boulder once more, her eyes on the land that stretched to the far horizon. She shifted closer to the ledge and sat with one leg drawn up, her hands folded over her knee.

He took a seat beside her, both legs hanging over the edge. "Can't put my boots on yet. It's too hard to tug them off. I need someone to help."

She cast a glance his way and said nothing. It hurt to see her quiet and withdrawn. He thought of that first meeting, her fiery brilliance perched on top of the roan, both of them blazing in the sun. Life. She was everything bright and good in life.

"Your dad told me about the baby carrier. If we could find out what store it came from, we might trace it to the person who bought it."

She was silent. He waited.

A frown nicked two little lines above the bridge of her nose. "Do you think so?" she asked hesitantly, worry invading her eyes.

The tension eased a tiny bit in his shoulders. He had her attention now. "Yes. I'll need assistance—"

She looked away.

"Someone to drive me to town or wherever we needed to go to check out this new clue, someone with a sharp analytical mind."

She swallowed and appeared minutely interested. But not convinced. Not yet. He had a long way to go to claim his love. He was willing to go however far it took.

"It would be something we could do while I'm recovering and you're working on your dissertation."

"Why should I want to work with you?" She laughed briefly, cynically. "Or more to the point, why should you want to work with me?"

"You know."

Her breasts moved as she took a deep breath. She wore a blue work shirt and jeans. Her hair was braided at the back of her neck, a blue bandanna wrapped across her forehead. She was indescribably beautiful.

She looked straight at him. "No. I don't know."

He touched her cheek, let his fingers wander over her temple and the tiny curls that wafted in the slight breeze rising from the gorge. "I want to start over."

"Start what over? Our casual affair? The fling?"

"You're not going to make this easy, are you?" He dragged one finger around the rim of her ear and marveled at how wonderfully she was formed, perfect in every way.

The frown smoothed out, but there was no glow, either. She simply watched him, as poker-faced as a cowboy in a bunkhouse game.

"I want…" He licked his lips. This was harder going than he'd bargained for. If he'd thought that by appearing she would leap into his arms and all would be fine, he had another think coming, as his old partner and friend would have told him.

Women, Stan had said, were funny little critters. They knew what was what. A man would be wise to listen.

"I'm asking for another chance," he finally admitted. He exhaled loudly, relieved to have gotten the words out. "I think I can get it right this time."

He waited.

The rusty door that had hidden hope from his distrust all these years opened a crack. He tried not to think of the boy who had been afraid to enter that room. He'd learned the hard way that letting hope in was opening the door to disaster. But for her, he had to take the chance...if she would let him.

He waited.

Vanessa tried to ignore the warmth that spread down her side and all the way through her at his closeness.

"Did my father put you up to this?" she finally asked.

Surprise darted through the heavenly blue eyes. "Hardly. Well, he suggested you might be at the stables. Cruz said you were probably up here."

She nodded jerkily. "It's embarrassing that everyone on the ranch is concerned about my love life." Her laugh was forced and more than a little cynical. "Or lack of same."

"They care about you. As I do."

"I don't know what you're asking...what you want from me."

Pain flickered in his eyes, but he smiled at her oh, so gently. "I want what we had and I threw away. I love you, Beauty. I can't get away from that."

Her heart stopped, then pounded furiously. The warmth blazed, died down, blazed anew. "But you want to?"

"Not anymore."

"You told me to leave."

"I know." He waited, letting her sort through his words and her emotions until she knew whether she could trust either. Trusting was hard. He knew that, too.

He touched her cheek, then hooked his finger under her chin and turned her to face him. He gazed deeply into her eyes, willing her to believe, needing that from her.

'I was wrong," he confessed. "Life can be uncertain—"

"But it can also be good," she murmured. "Someone I trusted once told me that the bad always passes."

"Trust him again," he requested.

She gazed at the cattle grazing in the meadows. She took in the clear, cloudless sky and the lengthening shadows of late afternoon. She watched a leaf tremble on a branch of an old oak. At last she looked at him.

"All right." She heard the uncertainty in her voice and knew he did, too.

"Okay, that's all I'm asking for now." He leaned back on an elbow. "You hungry? Cruz sent some hardtack."

She shook her head. "It's getting late."

"I don't think I'm up to sleeping on the ground tonight," he told her with a wry glance at the shallow cave. "Unless it's your most fervent desire."

She had to laugh. "Watch it, Mr. FBI man. A humble agent is a scary thing."

Standing, she held out her hand to him. He let her help him up. She led the way to the horses. Glancing at the roan, then him, she shook her head. Like Cruz, she bent and put her hands together and braced them on her knees.

"Okay," she said.

He stepped up, then swung onto the horse. She was aware of his gaze on her as she mounted and started down the trail at a careful walk. They spoke of the weather, how dry the grass was getting, when the rains would come, on the trip to the house.

Cruz met them at the stables. "I'll take care of the horses," he volunteered. He glanced at Dev. "You still her fiancé?"

Dev shrugged. "It's touch and go," he admitted.

Vanessa dropped the reins and stared at her nemesis. "Did you introduce yourself as my fiancé?" she demanded.

"Yes."

She was speechless. "Well, you have to ask first." With that, she walked off, not sure if she was angry, insulted or elated. After a couple of steps, elation won out. She couldn't believe she was being so foolish. She looked back at Dev. Her love. She smiled tentatively. He gave her a solemn smile in return. Her heart bounced a little.

Dev took her elbow and led her to his truck. He drove back to the main house and parked in his usual spot, then turned off the engine and rested his hands on the steering wheel.

"Wait," he requested when she started to get out. He cleared his throat. "I want the future. With you."

She pressed a hand against her heart, which beat like a drummer gone mad. "What kind of future?"

"Marriage. Will you marry this Beast and save him from a life of loneliness?"

She studied him. Did he feel guilty? No, his eyes held no guilt. A slightly anxious patience, perhaps, but not guilt. He was waiting for the word from her.

He touched one finger to her temple beside her eye. "I want the glow, Beauty. I want to wake up every morning and see those green eyes sparkling and teasing and full of life. I want a woman determined to give me hell...and heaven...and all the things in between. I want the woman who has haunted me for every hour of every day since I met her. That woman is you. Marry me."

His words were simple and beautiful. They fell into her heart like teardrops into a crystal pool, rippling through her soul the way a perfect phrase of music could.

She touched his cheek, his jaw, slid her fingers into his thick strands of hair. He was not perfect, but he was her love. A smile started inside her. It bubbled and frothed and welled until it burst out on her face.

"Yes," she said. It was a promise.

For a second he didn't move, then his arms closed around her. He pulled her against him in a fierce embrace, then he groaned.

She laughed and gave him a knowing look.

He gave her a disgruntled frown. "I'm not completely incapacitated," he warned her.

"I hope not," she murmured wickedly.

They climbed out of the truck and ambled arm in arm toward the house.

She basked in the heat of his gaze. "I suppose we had better go in and face my father. He'll be glad. He thinks I should have whatever I want." She glanced at her love to see how he took this outright fib.

To her delight, he laughed aloud. "He probably thinks you're making a mistake, but he's willing to let you learn from your own foolishness."

She put a finger over his lips. "Love may not always be wise, but it's never a mistake."

He stopped and gave her a solemn look. "It was foolish of me to deny the best thing to come along in my life. That day at the hospital and again at my house, I'm sorry for hurting you."

"You did it for me. I knew that...later, when I could think about it."

He kissed her then, a pledge to their future. His arms felt secure around her, his embrace big enough for her and their children, his heart strong enough for whatever came. They had found something good out of the tragedy of the kidnapping. They would build on that, a broad, brave foundation of love and trust and faith. Sometimes the darkness might knock at his soul, but love would drive it off. She could live with that.

He ended the kiss and smiled into her eyes.

"I think, my love, that the glow has invaded you," she observed softly, happily. She thought of all the things that needed to be done. "I have to call Victoria, oh, and Savannah. I'll need them for the wedding..."

Dev took her hand and started for the house once more. There was relief inside him. And yes, a glow. No matter how a person might mess up, some things did turn out right. And maybe, just maybe, a dream didn't always have to be beyond reach.

Here's a preview of next month's

THE FORTUNES OF TEXAS

*Sexy, swaggering Cruz Perez
comes face-to-face
with the beauty who is secretly carrying
his child in
EXPECTING...IN TEXAS
by
Marie Ferrarella*

"You came back."

Savannah Clark's stomach merged with her heart and both instantly raced for her throat. She wasn't sure which won.

Dressed in a black, embroidered Western jacket and a light blue shirt that made his complexion that much more romantically olive, Cruz Perez was standing behind her, a glass of punch in each hand.

It must have been her stomach that won the race, Savannah reasoned. Because her heart had stopped. Completely.

Cruz nodded toward the glasses, his smile unfurling like warm brandy sipped slowly on a cold day. "I seem to find myself with two glasses. Would you like to help me out and take one?"

She became aware that she was smiling in return. Widely. Savannah reminded herself that there was absolutely no reason for her to behave like a tongue-tied adolescent. Yes, he was beautiful, and yes, they had made love—wild, wonderful, passionate love together—but in the absolute scheme of things, that ultimately meant nothing.

Nothing, except that their night of lovemaking had produced a baby. A baby she wasn't ever going to let

Cruz know was his. Because she would never tie him to her. Not with bonds forged out of guilt.

Savannah inclined her head as she took the glass. "I guess I could, just this once."

She looked at the way the red punch caught the sun within it and gleamed invitingly. Almost as invitingly as his eyes had that night.

And now.

She raised her eyes to his. "And why wouldn't I come back for Vanessa Fortune's wedding? She *is* my best friend."

"No reason." He shrugged.

His eyes traveled over the soft contours of her face. Savannah felt as if he were actually touching her. "Except that you left so quickly the next morning. I thought that perhaps it was something I'd said. Or done."

His smile was so sensual, she struggled to keep her mind on the conversation.

Yes, it was something you'd done. You completely unraveled me, made me behave so that I didn't even recognize myself. And then made me want more.

Savannah took a long sip before she spoke, her throat suddenly too dry to even house dust.

"I had to get back." She purposely looked past his head as she spoke. "I had papers to grade. It was the end of the semester, the end—"

She stopped. Cruz was making her feel flustered and he knew it. She could tell by the look in his eyes. Why couldn't she just resist him? Be sophisticated like Vanessa or one of her other friends and just exchange teasing phrases? What was missing within her that seemed so plentiful in everyone else?

He moved slightly to stand in front of her, his brown eyes challenging her. "Tell me, Savannah, what am I thinking now?"

He'd never called her by her name before. It seemed to float to her on his tongue, making her feel even warmer than she already was. She was beginning to fervently wish that the bridesmaid dress had been sleeveless instead of having tight, long sleeves that ended a little over her wrists. Even if it had been sleeveless, she had a feeling that wouldn't help to cool her off.

After a moment she found her breath, although it wasn't easy. "That you'd like to dance with me." It was a wild stab in the dark, and probably wrong, but it was the only thing that came to her.

The deep, lusty laugh enveloped her as Cruz enjoyed her answer.

That was obviously not what had been on his mind. Was he remembering the moonlit night three months ago when they'd made love? Or was she alone in her memories...in her yearning?

"All right," he agreed amiably. "We can do that, if you'd like."

She'd been right. Dancing hadn't been on his mind. But she was afraid to think what had been. Afraid to think because she might be right.

More afraid because she might be wrong. And disappointed.

Taking the glass from her hand, Cruz placed it on the first available flat surface and gently took her into his arms.

Savannah felt like a princess. Just like the first time. She tried not to let the warmth of Cruz's body seep into hers. She might as well have made up her mind to take up permanent residence under the sea. It couldn't be done.

"I looked for you, you know. The morning after," he added when she looked up at him questioningly. "I was surprised that you had gone so quickly."

She'd gone because the reality of what she had done had suddenly hit her with the force of a two-ton truck. She'd been embarrassed and somewhat ashamed, as well. And more than that, she'd been afraid that he would laugh at her, at how easily he'd been able to seduce her. She couldn't have faced his laughter. Better to walk away with a lovely memory than to deal with aftermath and reality.

Except now she had to.

SPECIAL EDITION

Stories of love and life, these powerful novels are tales that you can identify with— romances with "something special" added in!

Fall in love with the stories of authors such as **Nora Roberts, Diana Palmer, Ginna Gray** and many more of your special favorites—as well as wonderful new voices!

Special Edition brings you entertainment for the heart!

SILHOUETTE®

Desire®

Do you want...

Dangerously handsome heroes

Evocative, everlasting love stories

Sizzling and tantalizing sensuality

Incredibly sexy miniseries like **MAN OF THE MONTH**

Red-hot romance

Enticing entertainment that can't be beat!

You'll find all of this, and much *more* each and every month in **SILHOUETTE DESIRE**. Don't miss these unforgettable love stories by some of romance's hottest authors. Silhouette Desire—where your fantasies will always come true....

DES-GEN

INTIMATE MOMENTS®
™ *Silhouette®*

If you've got the time...
We've got the
INTIMATE MOMENTS

Passion. Suspense. Desire. Drama. Enter a world
that's larger than life, where men and women
overcome life's greatest odds for the ultimate prize:
love. Nonstop excitement is closer than you
think...in Silhouette Intimate Moments!

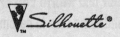

Silhouette®

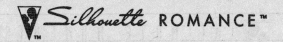
Silhouette ROMANCE™

What's a single dad to do when he needs a wife by next Thursday?

Who's a confirmed bachelor to call when he finds a baby on his doorstep?

How does a plain Jane in love with her gorgeous boss get him to notice her?

From classic love stories to romantic comedies to emotional heart tuggers, **Silhouette Romance** offers six irresistible novels every month by some of your favorite authors! Such as...beloved bestsellers **Diana Palmer, Annette Broadrick, Suzanne Carey, Elizabeth August** and **Marie Ferrarella,** to name just a few—and some sure to become favorites!

Fabulous Fathers...Bundles of Joy...Miniseries... Months of blushing brides and convenient weddings... Holiday celebrations... You'll find all this and much more in **Silhouette Romance**—always emotional, always enjoyable, always about love!